Praise for
A SABBATICAL IN

C000299400

'A book such as W.G. Sebald might have written, had he been an Irish engineer. In precise and penetrating prose, this novel probes memory and absence ... A quietly compelling work from a writer of real daring and poise.'

VONA GROARKE

'By turns poetic and forensic, exuberant and melancholy. At all times it is an entirely riveting, deeply felt musing on intimacy, loneliness and the nature of perception itself.'

SUE RAINSFORD

'There's a painstaking precision to the word and design of this book. Yet from such precision comes art. ... Slow, affecting and beautiful.'

NIAMH DONNELLY, *Irish Times*

'What I enjoyed so much about this beautiful, pensive book is how it made me look at the world differently.'

JUSTINE CARBERY, *The Sunday Independent*

'An entrancing read, one laced with despair, regret and tranquility ... It will be hard to forget this examination of time.'

ADAM MATTHEWS, *RTÉ Culture*

Praise for

LOVE NOTES FROM A GERMAN BUILDING SITE

'The best book I have read in years … a perfect depiction of love, and of desire and struggle.'

GREG BAXTER

'With elegance and precision, this beautiful book shows the forces that act on the structures of buildings and those that impact on relationships. Duncan's Berlin building site is, perhaps surprisingly, a brilliantly compelling place: the complications of construction converging with the complex experiences of those who work there.'

WENDY ERSKINE

'A strange, oblique, haunted work of quiet meditative intelligence. Adrian Duncan evokes the building of cities and the dislocated, phantasmal lives that unfold amid their looming geometries. His debut novel contains some of the finest writing on love I've read in recent memory.'

ROB DOYLE

'… a reflective, beautifully paced novel'

SARAH GILMARTIN, *Irish Times*

'If more men thought and wrote as tenderly and honestly, we'd have stronger, sturdier novels and fewer garish monuments to consumerism.'

DAVID O'CONNOR, *The Sunday Independent*

MIDFIELD DYNAMO

To Niamh

MIDFIELD DYNAMO

ADRIAN DUNCAN

THE LILLIPUT PRESS
DUBLIN

First published 2021 by
THE LILLIPUT PRESS
62–63 Sitric Road,
Arbour Hill,
Dublin 7, Ireland.
www.lilliputpress.ie

Copyright © Adrian Duncan

NOTE
This is a work of fiction. All characters, businesses,
objects-of-art, organizations and events portrayed
in this collection are either products of the author's
imagination or are used fictitiously.

The diagram that ghosts the contents page is like a
drawing one might see on a tactics board in a football
changing room. It shows one of many possible
patterns that underlie this book.

All rights reserved. No part of this publication may
be reproduced in any form or by any means
without the prior permission of the publisher.

A CIP record for this publication is available
from the British Library.

10 9 8 7 6 5 4 3 2 1

ISBN 978 1 84351 808 2

The Lilliput Press gratefully acknowledges the financial
support of the Arts Council/An Chomhairle Ealaíon.

Set in 12.5 pt on 17.5 pt Fournier by iota (www.iota-books.ie)
Printed by GraphyCems in Spain

Note to reader

The stories in this book are arranged into a starting eleven and a coach. I chose a field position for each story based on the personality I perceived from it. This layout helped me to visualize the book's elements, structure and possible patterns.

My team formation is the somewhat old-fashioned: 1-4-4-2. I've decided, also, to stay true to its numbering system, which is not altogether straightforward. For example, the left winger is given the number 11, one of the central midfielders is given the number 4 and one of the centre-halves has been numbered 6 ...

This layout, however, is not to suggest there is a preferred order for reading these stories. All I am hoping to say in describing my method is that this particular arrangement of stories is the one I most trust.

Team formation: 1—4—4—2

1.

Design No. 108

2. 5. 6. 3.

Houses by the Sea *Two Towers in a Forest* *Trusses* *Two Silences*

7. 4. (c) 8. 11.

Oregon Grape Tree *Midfield Dynamo* *Prosinečki* *Half Bird Half Bear*

10.

Forty-eight Pots of Honey

9.

We Too Have Wind-blown Plazas

Coach:

About the Weight of a Bucket of Salt

Kalugin fell asleep and had a dream: He's sitting in some bushes and a policeman is walking by.

Kalugin woke up, scratched around his mouth and fell asleep again, and again he had a dream: He's walking by the bushes, and in the bushes sits a policeman, hiding.

– 'A Dream', Daniil Kharms,
from *Today I Wrote Nothing*

DEFENCE

1

Design No. 108

When we were very young my brother and I used to stand in front of the window of our sitting room and peer out at the world. Our house, I should say, is pure *Bungalow Bliss*, straight from the book, design number 108, 'The Hazels'. Except for one tiny difference: the builders got the front living-room window all wrong. It is massive.

One night when my parents went out drinking all over town, a storm blew in. The wind grew to a thunderous roar. My brother and I looked out through the wobbling single-glazed window and we held each other tight. With one particular gust, the pane of glass bulged and burst in upon us. A whole world of dust, leaf, branch and tree surged in and gathered us up in a confounding swirl, wherein I could see my brother being hurled towards a mirror. He hit it head first then he fell to the floor, as did I. I clambered over to him and shouted through the gale:

'Are you serious, sir?'

He looked blankly back at me. A large shard of glass protruded from his cheek. I removed the glass, dragged him to the kitchen, closed all of the doors, pulled him onto the table, grabbed my father's chloroform cloth, knocked my brother out and operated on him. I cleaned the blood from his face, stitched his cheek together, rubbed saltwater into the wounds and left him there to rest.

Days later, with the wind still bellowing around our sitting room, I roused my brother and we left through the back door of our house into a calm and sunny autumnal day. We ran to the museum where we usually found our parents after their binges, my father passed out on the steps and my mother sitting bolt upright. My mother gathered my brother and I up into her bosom and held us close.

Many years from now, I will sit at my lamp-lit study desk and notice a large red blot of ink in my ledger – a blot absent-mindedly made with an old bingo marker unearthed from a box, after I had moved house, at the end of a lifetime of many painful divorces – and I will think of my dear brother's face.

•

When we were very young my brother and I used to stand in front of the window of our sitting room and peer out at the world. Our house, I should say, is pure *Bungalow Bliss*, straight from the book, design number 108, 'The Hazels'. Except for one tiny difference: the builders got the split-level floor joists all wrong.

My father, a builder and salt merchant, once came close to complete ruin. After many visits from a young bank manager whose manner was kind, my father was forced to sell his warehouses by the sea, his residential properties, all of his trucks, vans and lorries and most of his salt stock. What was left of the stock was deposited, one morning, outside of our house and covered over with a sheet of white plastic. My father spent four months in bed. The autumn day he chose to re-enter the world was so clear that I was sure he would cry when he saw it. But he simply sat at the kitchen table and drank a cup of steaming coffee, in a strange, deliberate manner. Eventually he called the family to the table and said:

'That, out there, under that tarpaulin, is all I have left.'

We turned and looked at the white quaking mound.

'Underneath that sheet of plastic is three tonnes of salt brick,' he said, 'and,' he said, 'we must get it indoors before the winter comes.'

The three tonnes of salt were stacked on the upper part of our split-level home where the builders had built the joists incorrectly. And, some creaking weeks later, the whole ziggurat of salt and timber and nail and dust came clattering down, crushing my dear brother, my mother and me. As for my father? I have no way of telling what he did next or where he went.

•

When we were very young my brother and I used to stand in front of the window of our sitting room and peer out at the world. Our house, I should say, is pure *Bungalow Bliss*, straight from the book, design number 108, 'The Hazels'. Except for one tiny difference: the builders, unpaid for weeks, decided to construct it with substandard blocks.

When my father noticed cracks all over the house he invited an engineer to carry out a survey. The engineer found the walls had been built with cavity blocks cast with a large percentage of salt in them, and were 'criminally substandard'.

Armed with this report my father and his solicitor tracked down the builders, and threatened to sue them 'into the ground'. They agreed to reconstruct the walls of the house inside the existing walls of salt block. I remember the hammering and churning and cursing and smoking around our abode, the strange men, their smells, their breath, their rough hands, the close quarters. The foreman on this job was handsome, and over the course of this rebuild my mother's appearance and manner changed. You don't need me to describe her lingering around the site, the flirting, the predictable exposure, the schism, the confusion, the unfinished walls of our house and my father's flight to the sea, his moon-glimmered thrashing, flailing, roaring, gulping, etc.

∎

When we were very young my brother and I used to stand
in front of the window of our sitting room and peer out at
the world. He would lean forward, touch the window with
his fingers and then count from one to one hundred – over
and over again, as if by doing so he could make the window disappear.

I would ask him to stop. He would ignore me; then we
would fight like small beasts until one of us bled.

'How is this sore for you?' the victor would cry. 'Tell me
now: how is this sore for you?'

∎

When we were very young my brother and I used to stand
in front of the window of our sitting room and peer out at
the world. Our house, I should say, is pure *Bungalow Bliss*,
straight from the book, design number 108, 'The Hazels'.
Each Saturday morning my brother, barefoot, would take
to the roof, and I to the attic. He would lasso around the
chimney pot a harness he had fashioned of rope and tyre
tubing. Meanwhile, just below in the attic, I would sit and
listen, and my mother beneath in the sitting room would
kneel at the hearth and begin building the house fire. My
brother would begin abseiling around the chimney, it by
now issuing skyward spirals of smoke from the fire in the
hearth of the sitting room below. Round and round my
brother would go thud thud thudding upon the clay tiles.

He, this great centrifugal god of the skies, while I, in the attic, listened. I watched the tiny haphazard dumps of dust falling down from the battens, felt and trusses each time his feet struck the roof – until these puffs of dust settled, all of them, in little piles upon the boards of the attic floor, among the toys and tat and rubbish. Then I would hear my brother sitting on the ridge tiles breathing heavily, and my mother would call up at me through the oblong of light in the floor of the attic, telling me I should come down for breakfast. I'd hear her go outside and call my brother down, but he would just tell her to 'do one'.

One winter's morning, the whole place crusted with frost, my brother's harness gave way and he slipped from the roof. For a moment he was exorbitant, untethered from the sky and the earth, until he landed in the yard on his head. He slept for ten months. On the afternoon he woke, he leaned over to one side of his bed and threw up into a gleaming metal bucket endless – thunderous – strings of blood-yellow bile. Then he lay back, closed his eyes and smiled, and the autumn sun, shafting across the galaxies of boiling dust, through the hospital blinds and onto his red glistening lips, bounced and finally came to rest upon the backs of my gaping eyes.

My brother then sat up and announced to us all that he could no longer smell anything, and that whatever invisible filament of connection to the world we all enjoyed, he no longer had it, or wanted it, and, he said, that he felt sorry for us all still so bound to the very things we wished to flee.

2

Houses by the Sea

My brother owns a second home by the sea. When I go there, I run most mornings along the beach; it curves for a mile or so until it comes to a small peninsula of black sea-slick crags.

One morning it was grey, misty and still. The waves broke and ran listlessly. It had not been raining, but the whole place was wet, as if a low-flying cloud had grazed along the coast and forgotten a piece of itself before it was pushed up over the mountains. On my way back I saw a piebald cow stuck knee-deep in the surf. It was struggling and looked as if it might topple at any moment. I chased over and tried to lead it out of the water, but it didn't want to go. I stood looking at it for a while, it looking calmly back at me. When its breathing eased I tried once more. I urged it back up the strand to the dunes, then onto some grass where the other cows were grazing.

As I walked back to the house, I looked over my shoulder and saw the cow again, shitting and lumbering back down towards the sea. I continued on a few steps, then turned and ran back. I stood in front of the cow, cajoling it back up the strand. We slowly zigzagged our way across the beach, back down once more towards the surf – me shooing, the cow changing direction – until I found myself stomach-deep in water and leaning against this animal's dark heaving chest. Then it pushed me over; I was submerged and sea-deafened. By the time I scrambled back to my feet, it was past me and almost up to its neck in water. I stood there shivering, with the waves breaking across me, and watched it disappear.

My brother's place, that he almost never uses, is on a hill outside a small coastal town. I come here to get away from my bedsit in the city. I left my wife a few years back for another woman. She and I then split soon after and she went back to her husband and two sons. I now find this part of the country hospitable. On the ragged strip of road that leads up to the house there are a number of other decrepit black-windowed bungalows, plopped hodge-podge down the hill.

In the town, which is probably more a village, there are two big hotels, a harbour, a shop and no pubs, so when I come here I call around to a guy called Leonard for a drink. He was once a priest, well educated, theology, history, that sort of thing – a PhD and a Master's degree from the

Sorbonne and Leiden, he told me. He's a decent guy, but he has completely given up. His wife passed away three years ago in their holiday home after she had been sick for a while. And he can't leave. First time I met him was by his front hedge; I was out for a walk and we began talking. He asked me in for a cup of coffee, six times. We ended up drinking whiskey and conversing all day.

It has been a few months since I've been here; so after I get back to the house and take a shower, I call up to him with a paper-bagged bottle of Jameson under my arm.

When he comes to the door, he looks at me for a moment and says, 'Finn.' It's almost a question.

'Leonard.'

He looks awful. His white hair has thinned, and his narrow face looks longer and somehow more drawn – as if, since I've last seen him, he has been hanging tiny weights from his skin.

'Come in,' he says.

The house is on the cusp of being left to waste. It certainly hasn't been cleaned, maybe since I last saw him. The corridor is poorly lit. The rooms off it are dark too. The pale carpet is worn and there is a smell of animal about the place.

We sit in his fluorescently lit kitchen and he makes us coffee.

'Good to see you,' he says, 'I was hoping you'd call up.'

I sit back into my chair and look around the kitchen listening to the thrum of the electrics, and the whoop of the sea wind outside.

'I wonder could you look at the house?' he says.

'Sure,' I say. 'Why?'

'Structurally,' he says, 'my solicitor tells me, to sell this place I need a certificate of compliance; I thought you wouldn't mind.'

'I can do that.'

He stirs his coffee gently, before taking another mouthful. Then he pushes the cup to one side and we open the whiskey and start to drink.

I tell him about the cow.

Many hours later, I wake up on the sofa in Leonard's sitting room. He has passed out and is breathing clumsily on the chair across from me. That glowing blue darkness you get just before dawn is everywhere, suggesting the shape of everything. We, glasses in hands, look like a couple of narcoleptics who dropped off mid-sentence. I lie back and close my eyes.

When I was much younger, twenty-two or so, I lived in the north of England for a number of years. I met a woman one night – she would have been over forty. We got drunk and went back to her place. She was rich, in that her parents were. In her bedroom she had a JD Fergusson portrait, depicting a dark-haired woman in a Parisian café. I loved that pink painting. This woman and I fucked each other all night. Next afternoon I hobbled home, empty. Every Friday night after that I'd get a call from her. She'd be drunk and ask me over. I'd always say I had no money – which was mostly true – and couldn't get across town. She'd say that she would take care of it. So when I'd roll up at her house in a taxi, she'd come out and pay, like she was my mother, then I'd go inside and fuck her in a cold way. She is the only woman I can say with certainty that I have ever satisfied.

Around this time I was drinking every weekend, to the point where I would black out on large chunks of the night. It was as if, when I was drinking, I would not ground myself. I would allow nothing to adhere.

I am awake again. It is morning and Leonard is standing over me.

'Finn,' he says, 'Finn.'

I rise and follow Leonard to the kitchen where we have a cup of tea and some toast. He reminds me of the survey. We finish our breakfast and, as we walk around the bungalow documenting cracks, I assure him there is no subsidence serious enough to compromise the sale. We enter the room where his wife spent her last few months. A neatly made single bed sits along the gable wall and the curtains are pulled. Around the room images of Catholic icons and rosary beads dangle from timber ledges holding various discoloured bottles of holy water. I scan the room for defects, make some notes and we leave.

In the hallway he pulls a folding stairs down from the attic and we clamber up to look at the trusses. The space is cold but dry, and the fibrewool between the trusses shines under the glow of a single bulb. From somewhere behind Leonard I can hear the gurgle of a water tank. As we hunker in among the criss-crossing roof struts, I feel like we are part of an intimate guild of joiners. I ask him why he is selling the place so suddenly.

'There's nothing sudden,' he says, 'I need the money is all. I'm six years from retirement, and I've nothing to get me there.'

'Where will you live?' I ask.

'I have a sister.'

'Where does she live?' I ask.

'Inland from here,' he replies.

The following weekend, the weather is bright and breezy and the smell of seaweed drifts almost visibly around the shoreline. I call up to Leonard. He meets me at the door – his wavy white hair standing on end, like a static charge has entered him. He is stone drunk and falling around the place, as if he has not stopped drinking since I left. I imagine the sadness; it opens before me like a Burren fissure, full of wild and rare flowers. The house is turned upside down, the kitchen has been destroyed and the windows in the sitting room smashed. He slumps at the kitchen table and offers me a can of cheap beer. I put the cert down, and tell him it's good to send to his solicitor. I understand, as he looks at me, that he has forgotten about the cert and that he has forgotten he wants to sell his house.

'Have you a cigarette?' he slurs. 'I couldn't find any fucking cigarettes.'

'Can we get some cigarettes?' he continues.

He can barely keep his head upright.

'I'll get them,' I say. 'You stay there.'

'Let me come,' he says, 'I need some air.'

I look at him and measure the difficulty in carrying him to the village. He peers at me through a hundred yards of mist.

'C'mon,' I say, and I get him to his feet.

On our way down to the village, after stumbling countless times, he falls on his face. His nose cracks. As I lift him blood pours from his mouth. His septum has shifted across a nostril. We sway on the side of the road about two hundred metres from the village harbour. It is windy, the sea froths behind us, and I picture how this could look. He begins to moan. His eyelids open, so I drag him back to his house and put him to bed.

Next morning I call up. He is sitting at his kitchen table with an open bottle of perfume in front of him. He's been sipping from it for I don't know how long. He begins to mumble something. It may be a psalm.

'I have told you these things, so that in me you may have peace. In this world you will have trouble. But take heart! I have overcome the world,' and he looks up, waves and says, with whatever finality he can muster, 'John, sixteen thirty-three ...'

He takes a sip from the bottle.

'I dreamt last night that I was bit by a dog,' he says, 'ferocious dream, must have been near the morning. The bite was so deep I woke up rubbing my arm. I jolted right off the bed, and fell. Then I felt my face, and wondered where it happened. So I searched the house for bloodstains, but found none. My face is in a terrible state.'

He rubs his chest, 'You wouldn't have a cigarette?'

I lift the perfume from the table and take a swig. I almost throw up. I put it back on the table and leave.

Next day, when I go to his house, Leonard is lying on his back on the floor of the kitchen. In the parting between his jumper and his corduroys I see his hip bones. They are coursed with blue veins throbbing like a snake that has eaten a large animal, one far too large for its own mouth, and the animal is curled up perishing among the snake's long organs. I leave, and when I get back to the house I call my office and tell them it might be a few days before I make it in.

Next day, the landscape feels empty, like the houses have returned to the rocks. I go to Leonard's. He is still lying on the floor, but has rolled his body into the recovery position. I survey the kitchen for any other signs of life.

Next day I call up to Leonard's once more. Some presses have been opened and a few condiments and a bag of sugar have been pulled to the ground. A broken drinking glass is by the patio doors. He is lying, barely breathing, on the floor. There is sugar across his sunken lips and mounded in one of his claws. I kick his legs and throw water on his face. I sit him up and try to get some sugared water down his throat. After a few distant clicks, he gulps, then gulps again, then retches. I carry him back down to his bedroom and lie him in his bed. I ring an ambulance and when they arrive I tell them that I call up to visit him every now and then, and that I found him this morning in a terrible state on the kitchen floor.

5

Two Towers in a Forest

The walls of the terraced house in which I live are constructed with red brick. The house has a pitched slated roof, timber floors and two upstairs bedrooms. The front bedroom, where I sleep, faces out onto a square. Some nights this square can become quite noisy: dogs barking, distant helicopters, horses pounding stable doors, sirens, speeding cars, shouting ... and on these occasions I push two old wax earplugs into my ears to drown out the sound. Then, lying there in bed, I begin to hear the blood pumping behind my ears, and I think of my grandfather, whom I never met, who died of a heart attack over seventy years ago while playing cards one afternoon with his young wife and his sisters at the kitchen table of his farmhouse, now derelict, that overlooks fields and a lake in the middle of the country. Then I think of the inherited weakness I must have in my heart and of the possibility that my heart will suddenly, violently stop, which causes me to think, what if my heart gives in as I sleep? and what is this pulsing object within me? and how can it truly be an object when it is part of me? And all of this confusion rehearses itself in my mind, over and over, until eventually it ebbs away in cascading throbs until I fall asleep and wake the next morning, exhausted, wondering what all the fuss was about.

I work as a draughtsman in a large bright engineering office. We design houses, bridges, churches and libraries. The engineers give me their hand-drawn sketches and I work them up into large formal drawings for issue to site. I sit beside another draughtsman. His name is Allen; a tall man, with blue eyes and a dark full beard. We both began working here on the same day, ten years ago – a clear Monday morning in August 1978. Allen and I consider the engineers in this office as artless types. We work our handsome tracing-paper drawings up in pencil, and neatly ink in these lines, then, if the engineer spots a mistake in the design, we have to take our razor blades out and scratch away the dried-up lines of ink and redraw the correct plan area, the cross-sectional detail, the note, the specification – and the drawing is ruined. I often become quite angry and lose interest in the project at hand.

I am an only child. Once a month I go home to visit my mother, who lives in a council cottage at the end of an old cul-de-sac in the Midlands. My mother is beautiful. She has long dark hair even though she is quite elderly, and eyes so black it is a wonder she can see out of them. She feels alone these days and cries whenever I mention anything from the past. She misses my father, who died forty years ago, two years after I was born, while he was working as a welder on a Dutch vessel exploring for oil in the middle of the North Sea. It is my wish to make her happy again, to help her forget about the past for a moment, and with this task in mind I have begun work on a large project. It is to be built in the belly of a patch of forest that was once bequeathed to her. The forest is full of upright and fallen trees, and it smells almost of decay. I think it will die very soon – it will in a sense strangle itself to death. Before this happens I want to build two towers in the forest. Then I will bring my mother to see these towers, at night, when they are both lit up by dozens and dozens of high-strength lamps.

The day I moved into my terraced house I dismantled the two single beds in the spare bedroom upstairs, turning it into a studio for this project. Every moment I am not working in the engineers' draughting office, I spend in the spare bedroom working on one of the towers – a ziggurat, more precisely. I will build it in balsa wood, in 360 interlocking parts, then I will transport the tower, piece by piece, to my mother's patch of forest. It is a plot of 4.2 acres, and in the centre of it is a large concrete pad once used for storing silage. Upon that eight-hundred-square-metre pad I intend to assemble, to its thirty-metre height, the ziggurat.

The dimensions have been carefully considered so that the internal and external surface areas of my ziggurat will approach one one-millionth of the surface area of my mother's patch of forest in mid-summer. By surface area I mean the area of each side of each leaf, each branch, each bole, each piece of grass, plus that of the ground these groaning things emerge from. On a number of visits to the forest last June, Allen and I – with measuring tapes, metre-square sheets of tracing paper, ladders, pulleys, rope, climbing gear, cameras, notebooks – carried out a survey of the place. The plot has on average one deciduous tree in every two square metres; the average height of a tree is 8.2 metres; the average trunk diameter is 311 millimetres. My calculations factor in the unevenness of the bark of the tree trunks and the smoothness of the branches. The average length of the secondary branches is 3.5 metres, the average number of secondary branches is forty-five per tree, the average number of leaves on each branch is fifty-six. The average leaf area on 22 of June last year, from a test sample of two hundred leaves, was 83.2 square millimetres. Grass: at the edges of the forest the blade count was 413 per square metre, the average area of one side of each blade was 12.5 square centimetres. In the inner parts of the forest the average blade count per square metre was 126, the average area of one side of each blade was 8.3 square centimetres. Moss: the area of moss was assumed to sit within the tree area and the forest-floor area. Flowers and miscellaneous weeds: add .05% of the area of grass.

From this Allen and I produced colour-coded maps relating to each of these layers of the forest so we could iterate its entire surface area in summer and, from this, discern – taking away the leaves and a percentage of the grasses – the area in winter.

Which leads me to the second tower: I intend to purchase a giant roll of electric-blue stage light film, the surface area of which will tend towards one one-millionth of the area of this same forest plot, mid-winter. Allen and I will go to a clearing in another part of my mother's plot, unfurl this roll of film across the ground and, using a number of simple geometric propositions – each corner curled to the midpoint of the opposite edge – bend the material over and upon itself over and over, repeating these rules until the sheet, through its sheer stiffness, stands upright. At night I will install and shine huge stage lights through this unsure object, and disclose, through a build-up of electric-blue tone, the curved structure.

In the end I will have two huge sculptures sitting in different places in my mother's forest, with surface areas that are relative to the difference in the forest between summer and winter, and expressed using my two preferred types of geometry: the grid-like units of the Cartesian, and the continuous surface curves and bends of the Topological.

Allen at first did not believe in this project, but the more I talked with him about it during our lunch breaks at work, and showed him my drawings and my corrugated cardboard models, and impressed upon him just how important I felt the project was and who it was for, the more he took to it, to the point that he became enthusiastically involved. He began calling over to my apartment more often to see how the models and designs were progressing and offering often to double-check my calculations. In short, this project has brought us from being mere workmates to 'brothers-in-arms', as he often says. One evening in the early stages of construction, we were driving to the hardware suppliers in the middle of the small Midlands town not far from my mother's house. I needed to purchase some lengths of pine as supports for my sheets of balsa. As we went, and the distant street lights began to wink on the horizon, he turned to me and said, as if he had been considering this detail of the project for some time, but had been afraid to ask, '... And why balsa?'

To which I replied, 'Workability and fragrance.'

The day we lifted into place the peak of the ziggurat, Allen stood and looked out over the top of the forest. The tips of the trees bobbed around us in a slow asynchronous way, and the ziggurat creaked gently below. It was a warm and sunny afternoon and all of the different scents of timber coursed up through the air. Allen placed his left foot onto the top step of the ziggurat and stood astride it for a while, like a mountaineer, gazing out over the land. He held this posture, closed his eyes and breathed deeply in through his nose, then out through his mouth, a number of times, until it became obvious that standing like this was tiring him out and his thighs, knees and calves were beginning to strain. The birds chirped nearby and the flies cut spiralling curves down into the sparkling forest below. Allen opened his eyes, took out his pouch of tobacco, rolled a cigarette, smoked it and sent a string of ragged grey-white hoops out into the heavens – they wobbled then expanded into obliteration. I took a seat on the top step of the ziggurat, and looked out over the tips of the trees, the farmland beyond, the lake, the distant hill.

Then, Allen uttered: 'I think we have done something very fine here.'

I did not respond.

He asked me when I hoped to light up the forest and show these two giant constructions to my mother, and I said that I would do it as soon as I got some more lights and more generators to power them. I told him that he should not worry because I would certainly take him back here some day, before it all rots, or is blown asunder.

∎

And this is where I am now, in the middle of a very dark night, in my van, hurtling with my mother to this godforsaken plot of forest. We have gin, blankets and food. We roll up to the forest entrance and I insist on blindfolding her. She is nervous and hesitant as I lead her through the damp darkness and halfway up the side of the ziggurat. As she and I falter up the steps she asks me what on earth it is I am doing. I sit her down, and tell her not to move and that she must leave the blindfold on until she hears me call for her. I excuse myself, chase down into the trees to start the generators, to power the stage lights that will illuminate my vast curling electric-blue film sculpture. The generators click, groan, hammer, whirr. Then the lights slowly come up, and the whole forest begins to glow and oh ... it is glorious – the forest is blue-ness: blue lines, gleaming blue curves and shapes that break in senseless arcs across the trees, the branches, the leaves, the glowing sap. The blue light quakes up through the dark undergrowth, the branches, the leaves until it blasts outward, obliterating the sky, way, way up, where it rolls and radiates and sings, and I start to shudder and run through all the blinding gunk, strand and shadow, and call from the top of my irregular heart:

'Mother! Mother! Come see what I have done!'

6

Trusses

I am lying on my back, staring up at the galaxies of damp spiralling across my bedroom ceiling. It is Wednesday. My wife, Eleanor, died thirteen months ago and I am still struggling for habit and will. My youngest child, Samantha, a purposeful woman, visits me twice a week, Tuesdays and Thursdays, on her way to veterinary college, and during those calls the bottom half of the house fills with warmth. Elizabeth, my eldest, whom I visit irregularly, lives in a fine semi-detached house in a pleasant part of Dublin city with an attentive husband and two vibrant children. My eldest son, Allen, lives in the next county over, but I have seen him only twice since Eleanor's funeral. He says that he can't bear the house without her sounds in it. I can't bear my bed without her small feet in it. Then there is Foster, my youngest son, who works as an engineer in Abu Dhabi and has not been home in three years. Recently, he has written a series of terse letters to me, talking about his work and his accommodation. There are only glimpses of heat in his notes, but these are enough to tell me that he has developed an unhealthy hatred of this country and is becoming unwell. He never asks after me or Allen or the girls, or mentions his mother. I received another letter yesterday, telling me he wants to become a writer, not as a career, but so as to 'invent routes out of my subconscious,' he says. He was the last to move out, and I often wonder what effect this had on him – living in this bungalow watching his siblings leave him to it.

Every morning, these days, I wake to the same memory. Eleanor and I – when we first had Elizabeth – would often meet on workday afternoons for tea in a small bright café in the middle of town. Elizabeth, who was a beautiful and quiet child, would lie there, then sit, then stand and talk and point at things. I had begun studying at the nearby technical college for a diploma in management, and my hours at the plant – where I spent all my working life – had to be shared with my study time and it sometimes left me less organized. One afternoon, I forgot about our usual arrangement to meet in the café. When I got home that night, Eleanor, who was pregnant then with Allen, told me that Elizabeth had missed me, that she'd stood on the sofa by the window of the café for a whole half hour, looking out the window and speechlessly wondering where I was. Next day I was coordinating a delivery of four two-tonne spools of copper wire to Dublin. After I'd waved off the loads I went inside, sat at my small desk in my cramped cold office and was overcome, for a moment, with a feeling of wretchedness for having somehow conspired to place such a delicate point of awareness into the vast expanse of my daughter's mind.

My hands are cold. I should get out of bed and light a fire or else I'll smother myself in these maudlin thoughts. The damp patch in the ceiling is so bad I can see right through to the underside of the timber truss. This whole ceiling will need to be repaired. Perhaps the roof felt is rotten too.

I should call Carl for some help. It's been forty years since we built this house, and fifty since we sat in the same classroom. The last time I saw him was on the street in town a few weeks after Eleanor, Elizabeth and I had moved in, and he told me he was emigrating to Boston. I remember being surprised and a little hurt that he had not even mentioned the possibility of making such a move during our time building the house together.

There was one hot afternoon when we were taking a break on the ridge of the roof, the angular planes below us almost fully patterned out in waves of brown and dark-brown tiles, and as he rolled up a cigarette and smoked it, he asked me if I had ever considered leaving. I told him, as the breeze frisked his short blond hair, that I had not. I probably said something like, 'Sure what more would you want?' We had played soccer together for years, so we were more or less shunned by the Gaelic footballers in the town – 'the devout savages', as Carl called them. That hazy afternoon sitting on the ridge of the roof we could see that the two large chimney stacks of the new factory, being carefully constructed on the outskirts of the town, were almost complete; and the tower cranes either side were beginning to descend, in folds. Carl finished his cigarette, flicked the stub toward a rusted barrelful of water in what would eventually become a flower bed and surveyed my plank-strewn site. I feel sure I saw in his face then the faintest flicker of boredom, but at the time I thought nothing of it, and merely suggested we finish out the roof.

I get up, shower and walk through the house to the kitchen, light the range and the living-room fire and drive to the filling station to buy some sausages and a news-paper. When I get home I fish my black phonebook out of a bottom drawer in the living-room dresser. Old colour photographs of Eleanor and me on a package holiday in Spain spill out – shiny waves of dated yellows, reds and blues. I flick through the phonebook and find a number for Carl's sister. I dial the number but it does not ring so I try a friend of a friend, Patrick, who, last I heard, had left the construction trade to buy a large pub in Ballsbridge. I call the pub, get his mobile number and call him, and for almost a minute he has no idea who I am. I tell him I am looking for our old friend Carl Jones, and he falls silent, apologizes and tells me that Carl moved home from Boston eight years ago, set up a demolition business, but passed away a few years later. He tells me it was a stroke, but there is some-thing uncomfortable in the way he says it. I ask if Carl had married, and Patrick gives me a number for his wife, Nance, an American lady whom he believes still lives in their home somewhere in County Westmeath.

I call Nance and Carl's number. The phone rings many many times. I eventually talk with a woman I assume to be Nance and tell her who I am. She enquires as to how I knew Carl, so I tell her we went to school together and that he helped to build my house. When I ask if I may call over, she says, 'Of course.'

Next day is showery and bright and I'm driving through the rolling farmland of Westmeath. The directions Nance gave me were vague, but she seemed quite certain I would find the place: 'It is a fine big old house,' she said.

The land opens. The tall hedges either side of the road splay, thin out and are replaced by cut-stone walls drawing adamant lines on the countryside. It has stopped raining and the sunlight has reached back around the dissipating clouds; the shadow of the wall aligns with the curves of the road as I go. The land rises around me and I see their house – an old misshapen three-storey thing that sits with what seems like an unearned regality about a quarter-mile in from the road. It is surrounded by small trees and undulating pastures. As I drive up the bumpy and threadbare entranceway I notice a row of dilapidated stables to the rear. At the front there's a new conservatory extension, populated with two large sofas, some wicker chairs, lamps, patterned throws and tall well-cared-for plants. A newspaper collapses and a woman's head appears over the back of the couch. I get out of my car as Nance comes to the conservatory door. She opens it and stands there: 'You must be Liam.'

'I am,' I say.

Nance is a small person, with short dyed dark hair. As we enter the bright conservatory and sit down, it becomes clear that Carl never spoke to her of me, or that she has forgotten whatever he might have said, and so I give her an account of our friendship. Nance then describes to me how she and Carl met in Boston, how handsome and energetic he was. She tells me about where they lived, her career as a pharmacologist, their three children and how Carl's business grew through the eighties and nineties until he received an enormous contract as part of the 'Big Dig', to knock and excavate a quarter-mile of Boston's downtown. 'That contract paid for this house,' she says in her soft New England accent. She is intelligent and effusive, and as she speaks I try to imagine her and Carl together, but I cannot.

Then I look at her, and I ask how it was Carl died.

She falls silent and her light-blue eyes become tearful. Then, gesturing, she tells me that once they came back here and he began working again he unravelled: 'And with all of the kids still in Boston getting on with their lives,' she says, 'he began to feel "rudderless".' To which she pauses and I can hear the ticking of a clock from somewhere in the adjoining hallway.

I peer around at the decorative Victorian style of the room and say to her that I would have gladly visited.

She looks at me, and puts one hand into the palm of the other. Then she brings me to a framed photograph on a piece of wall between two windows facing out onto the lush shining fields beyond. The photograph depicts a giant digger on a dusty street, framed out by a twinkling Boston skyline. On the flank of the digger are printed the words 'Jones Works' in dynamic green-and-black capitals.

While she looks to the photograph she tells me that once his work in Ireland dried up he had to let all of his employees go, 'and this hurt him,' she says. Then she tells me that to stem this hurt he took on himself any jobs that did come in 'with the last of his machines', and she looks down at her hands – she strikes me as a person who looks at her hands often – and then she says, her voice gently wavering, 'I'd ask him to let someone else do those jobs … but he'd just round on me and tell me he'd not sit in a dead office all day.'

She turns from the photograph as if it hurts her to look at it for too long, and she describes to me that, near the end, Carl had begun fixating on 'innocuous things' around the house – 'the trees, the shrubs, the ditches' – and that he didn't eat or sleep well … 'I'd often hear him pacing up and down the stairs at night,' she says.

Nance then asks me to follow her through the house, which is dark in the way of thick rubble-walled houses of this vintage. She leads me back to the kitchen window and points to a small hill on the brow of which is the lower third of a tree that was once a fine chestnut or sycamore or oak, something expansive, old and lung-like.

'That's where he had his stroke,' she says, and she then explains to me how one afternoon when she was out, that Carl, with his wrecking ball, had tried first to demolish the stables before he had a go at this tree, and that he was eventually come upon by their neighbour, a farmer, 'a nice man called Mr Holland,' she says, 'who was driving past when he found Carl slumped over the steering wheel, with the tree bent in two and the engine puttering out.'

I look at the tree trunk and imagine Carl up there swinging this enormous metal ball at it, trying to get purchase on the thing, and I begin to smile; then my smile broadens until I almost chuckle. I cough and try to look the other way before I give myself up and really laugh out loud, but I need not have been concerned, Nance is already laughing quietly beside me, she has the back of her hand to her mouth and her eyes are streaming, but she is certainly laughing, and this sets me off – I guffaw, I cackle, and Nance is shaking as if suppressing some prodigious mirth. I realize that she is very handsome laughing like this, but then her hand comes away from her mouth and her face contorts, and from her mouth comes a full broad howl and by now we are both not so much laughing as ululating, bent over double, like two wind-up toys bellowing out horrible demented shrieks that echo around the kitchen, to the point where I, for a moment, have forgotten what exactly I am laughing at, and I am afraid that one of us will die, or that I will accidentally urinate, or worse, that we will stay in this kitchen laughing in this convulsed fervour forever, gulping brutally for breath, so I take a hold of a chair that I can barely see, to try to steady myself, but also hoping that the inanimate object will somehow neutralize this surging elation. I grab the back of the chair with both hands, as hard as I can, until I see the ten whites of my knuckles before me and I dare not look away from them until I can feel our laughter falter and stop.

We pull ourselves together, and the world subsides once more, and Nance, who now looks strangely calm, as though she has been quietly watching me laugh alone all this time, hands me a glass of water, like a dental nurse would a patient, and I drink from it, and we look back out the window. I breathe deeply for a number of minutes, and after some time, just before I begin to feel very tired, I ask her might she ever return to Boston.

She chooses not to answer.

We stand in the quiet midday glimmer of the kitchen for a while looking out at the tree stump and the wet green hill and the birds whirling around and descending onto the electricity wires that draw drooping parallels over the base of the hill and beyond.

'Do you have a photograph of him?' I ask.

'I do,' she says, 'lots.'

'Could I have one, do you think?'

'Of course,' she replies.

That evening, when I arrive home, I am reminded that it is Thursday: there is a note from Samantha on the table, a single blue question mark written on the back of an electricity bill. I light a fire then call her and tell her I was seeing some friends, and I take the silence on the other end of the phone to indicate that she is about to ask me 'which friends', but instead she tells me about her coursework and that she has a birthday card for Allen's wife that I should sign. She says she'll see me on Tuesday, and then she's gone.

As I make a ham-and-cheese sandwich I think about Foster and how I struggle to imagine his predicament off out east in Abu Dhabi. So I sit and write a short letter to him. I tell him about Carl, how I knew him and how he died, and I enclose the small photograph of him in the envelope, in the hope that Foster might intuit something for himself from Carl's demise, or at least, in my writing this letter he will know that I still care for him.

When I first saw this photograph, while standing with Nance in their shadowy hallway, I found myself expanding my memory of the shape of Carl's young face into the form of the face in the photograph, a healthy middle-aged tanned and happy face, with thinning hair and the same blue eyes I think I remembered from the street in town. Time in that moment sullenly revealed itself as an invisible truss, spanning between moments; but I have now lost interest in what is propping it up. I seal the small envelope, address it and lean it against the sugar bowl in the middle of the table to remind myself to post it in the morning.

3

*Two Silences: One from the front and
one from the back of my head*

1. A buried forest of ferns

Once, a shelter to protect soldiers from falling rocks was
commissioned, designed and built for an army barracks in
Gibraltar. It was an oversized concrete pergola for officers
to walk under to take some air. The engineers charged with
designing the shelter found it a strenuous undertaking. The
most pressing questions at the outset were: at what height
might the largest rock fall from? What weight might that
rock be? And what then might be the force at impact? It
proved impossible for the engineers to calculate to a satisfac-
tory degree of rigour. They made site visits to the barracks,
carrying out desk studies of the tectonic and recent geolog-
ical history of the place. They made models; they developed 3D computer versions of the location too – clunking

animated dodecahedrons bounced down dark dimensionless terrains – then, exasperated, the engineers invited a team of statisticians to examine the probability of great movement in the landscape, but nothing would allay their fears of under-design. They settled instead on the army's codes of recommendation for bomb shelters and designed the structure for medium-range enemy ballistics.

For years, the rocks – great irregular igneous things – would fall and deflect off. Then the shelter outlived its design life and the sea air infiltrated the concrete and attacked the reinforcement within, rusting and expanding it, and causing the surface of the concrete to chip, break and spall.

The army decided to patch the shelter up, and the day the local contractor, a young man called Alvaro, began his repairs to the roof, a large rock came loose from the top of the hill behind. It tumbled down the ragged syncline and, missing him by inches, thudded horribly against the edge of the roof. The rock cracked open. One half keeled over and thumped dustily to the ground while the other yawned back onto the roof and wobbled there for many moments like a giant upturned turtle. Gathering himself, Alvaro spied in the centre of the rock a delicate index of a fossil of a fern, and in the midst of this ancient cyanotype was a white drawing of an insect's skeleton caught mid-flight between the fronds of the fern.

What a pretty and serene scenario that must once have been, Alvaro thought, as he mopped his brow. He pushed his thinning dark hair away from his eyes and squinted skyward at some circling birds; then, feeling an unearthly rumble developing behind him, he turned to a deluge of black rocks galloping down the hill. He leapt from his ladder and dived under the shelter. As these small planets pummelled overhead, bouncing off the roof and pounding emphatically onto the soil beyond, Alvaro wondered if all of these rocks were carrying in their centres such beautiful stilled moments as the one he had just spied, and if so has a forest of ferns ever made such a racket, and, he wondered, if this might have been how it once rained on the earth – giant thundering drops hammering the undergrowth of his paleolithic psyche.

Once the tip of the hill had all but slumped itself onto the shelter, the place fell quiet and Alvaro emerged, covered in dust and dirt and grit. As he clambered onto the roof of the shelter – to survey the new embankment of boulders below, all the while carefully patting himself down – a small rock, about the size of his shoulder blade, dislodged itself from the top of the hill. It skipped down frivolously, hopped, flew, then arrowed straight at the back of his head. One crescent of a second later with the army officers running out in file and horseshoeing around the shelter, Alvaro, with a clop, spun like an acrobat in a circus, flipped a three-quarter circle and landed on his back – his head two Janus-like crania, one of bloodied bone the other of gleaming calico. With a trickle of blood emerging from the corner of his mouth, he, before all of his thoughts disgorged into stillness, thought one final thought: 'This heat, this work, this dreadful salt and dust ...

tonight I'll drink that cool bottle of beer; it is somewhere in the back of the fridge beside the cherry tomatoes.'

Four junior army officers carried Alvaro's body back into their mess. He was brought home, tidied up, then buried in a cemetery outside of town. The shelter was decommissioned and eventually the barracks closed. Much later again the army abandoned Gibraltar, and the lands, with little ceremony, were given back to Spain.

Centuries from then, and after many further rockfalls, the shelter was completely covered over, buried under many tonnes of rocks and soil, and the landscape around it was altered too. In the shelter's new subterranean world it finally came apart completely, the last few columns disintegrated and the reinforcement within crumbled into mere piles of red filings, and with them, almost with a sigh, the last shreds of the engineers' concerns disappeared from the face of the earth.

2. Twelve beaches way off the coast of Portugal

I once worked as a sound recordist on mid-budget independent films. While I was working on these projects I used to often disappear for a day or two, at the end of each shoot, and make my own set of field recordings. Then I developed tinnitus in my right ear and had to leave the industry. I retrained as an engineer.

One night last week I worked until almost five, overseeing a concrete pour on a site – a soon-to-be printing works – miles outside of town. I woke early the next morning, and unable to get back to sleep I took to the couch in the sitting room of my apartment in central Dublin, listened to the traffic and dozed. When I am tired like this the distant ringing sound of my tinnitus often reappears and causes me discomfort. I could tell on that morning that if I didn't get some rest I would be revisited by this sickly feeling of noise. Then, while I was lying on my couch in my apartment I thought, for the first time in years, about a particular group of recordings I'd made over the course of a changeable day on a broad beach a few miles east of Carvoeiro, a town in southern Portugal not far from the Spanish border. I was in a low mood when I made them because my tinnitus had got so bad that I knew I couldn't trust myself to work in the industry much longer.

I rose from my couch, went to my desk and searched my laptop for these recordings; then, having found them in an old folder, I hooked my laptop up to my amp and speakers and set up these twelve recordings so they played in a relaxing continuous loop. I reclined on my sofa and closed my eyes.

The rhythmic churning of the sea waves came up, filling my sitting room with sound. I opened my eyes, then closed them once more and with this I fell into somnolence as the pace and intensity of the waves grew and fell and at times hushed in long barely audible crashes. The twelve tracks began morphing into something complete but whose distinct parts I was still able to discern. As the gentle shifts in tone and duration of each track clarified, an irregular dodecagon-shaped island in the middle of a twinkling ocean gradually took form in my mind's eye. The island was more an absence framed out by twelve edges of frothing white waves breaking around and over it. I watched this dark island pulsating there below me, the water bending into the black at its centre, as if these fabricated flows were themselves being swallowed forever by time.

In the fourth track – a five-minute recording made at midday when the sea at that beach near Carvoeiro must have been very still – I noticed the sound of a machine in the distance. I didn't remember hearing a machine while recording it. I listened errantly, waiting for the track to loop around again, and each time this track came round, this sound became more prominent, to the point that I soon found myself focussed on it entirely, separating it, then amplifying it in my mind until it drew me mathematically away from this trembling twelve-sided absence in the sea and towards the screaming source of this whine, and with this my mind's eye arrived at the oil-rig design classes I took many years ago while in university in Aberdeen.

I pictured my lecturer, a thick-set balding man with an American accent, moving in super slow-motion, his arms and hands blending into gestures made towards a blackboard, he informing us in a profound and sonorous voice of the problems that emerge when the frequency of the sea wind and waves and the natural frequency of an oil rig, sitting in among them, became resonant with each other. He'd walk over and back in front of this blackboard, covered in chalk scribbles, arrows, geometrics and glyphs, stating that this resonance was a sign of considerable danger, because if the frequency of any wave at any time or any gust of wind matched the natural frequency of any part of the oil rig – a beam, a column, a derrick – then this element would fall into a dangerous oscillatory vibration that required special welds and bolts to control. He said, if you missed one of these instances, the entire structure and everyone on it would be in great danger, and if anything drastic happened, it would be your fault and you would be charged in court, he would say slowly, with manslaughter.

When he lectured in this calmly macabre way, I'd dream later those nights of a young man sleeping in his bunk on an oil rig. This young man would start awake in the middle of the night to the sound of something whining, breaking, followed by a shunt, and his stomach flipping with panic. And in my recurring dream he'd lurch from his bunk and chase to the green exit light above the bunk-room door, but before he'd get there he'd be taken to the ground by one of his roommates, a senior rigger, who'd pin him to the cold metal floor and sit on him, and the young man would gyrate wildly underneath the older man, trying to flee, and the larger older man would smack the younger man in the face and whisper to him, 'You are dreaming again, please wake up, son, before you wake the others too. You know there's still a tonne of welding to do on the north leg, so go back to bed and quit this fucking around, son, and sleep, and don't worry; this thing is going nowhere. Now, are you okay? Are you tranquil? Are you going to go back to sleep?' And the younger man would nod, tears streaming down his face, and the older man would say into the crying man's ear, 'Good lad, don't worry – you'll be back again on the mainland in a few days.'

Then, the older man would lead the younger man, shivering, back to his bunk and tuck him in.

He'd return then to his own bed where sleep would eventually come to him too, but only in those deep and dark places plumbed most deeply and darkly in the moments just before he woke again in the morning.

MIDFIELD

7

Oregon Grape Tree

Every morning I take a tram into town. The carriages are always full of ghosts, their morbid lovers and lawyers. I find it a hurtling distressing journey.

This morning, finding it too much, I disembarked three stops early and walked the rest of the way into town. I visited the pound shop for a fan to blow air onto an Oregon grape tree I'd purchased a few days before. I want to look at how the tree – it's prickly and about three feet tall – will respond if I fasten all its leaves to these dozen or so lab stands I've positioned around it. One leaf will remain unrestrained. The response of the tree to these conditions will appear through the bobbing of the free leaf; and it is these movements I am curious to see.

I ambled over to an ancient flower seller on the corner and asked for a clay pot of begonias.

'Okay, love,' she croaked, and as she turned I grabbed a rose and ran and ran until I got home. I put the rose into a pint glass of water, and put the pint glass of water onto the middle of my kitchen table, and, while sitting there in the shafts of late-morning light – considering the crimson petals slowly coiling out towards me – I thought two things:

1. This *is* beauty. Yes?
2. Eat the flower.

So I ate the flower till my mouth bled.

Then I drank the water and went to bed and dreamt of my great and unforgettable love, Margaret, who had black hair, green eyes and a long and graceful neck.

•

When I rouse it is dark. I wander into the next room and turn on my lamps. I fine-tune the arrangement of my tree, my lab stands and my many clasps. I hook the tree up and turn the fan on. The tree just shivers, except for the free leaf, which oscillates happily in the air. I shine a lamp onto the leaf, pin a sheet of graph paper to the wall behind it and track the shadow of the leaf tip with my pencil. The line I draw is patternless but quite beautiful. I place the sheet into a folder, produce another sheet and place it behind the leaf, turn on the fan and trace another line, then another, then another, then another. Again, all patternless but quite beautiful.

I get the tram into town the next morning. It is full and smashes into some cars and a bus. People spill out onto the footpaths and road, some shaking, some holding their heads. I continue on foot to the call centre where I work. I sneak into my cubicle, take out the *Golden Pages* and begin to dial.

That evening, while sitting at home on my tiny settee, smoking a cigarette and watching the evening news, my phone rings.

'John,' I say, 'how're you, mucker?'

'Good good,' he replies. 'Thinking of making a trip down the country on Saturday, if ye fancy …?'

I ask him where.

'The centre of Ireland,' he declares.

'There is a centre?' I say, through a plume of smoke.

'I've wanted to go for years,' he says.

It is the following Saturday and John and I are driving around warrens of country roads trying to find the tower of stones that, he tells me, marks the centre of Ireland.

He takes a corner and accelerates up a hill. The land undulates alongside us as the sun flickers through the hedges.

John is married and has two young children. He is a good few years older than me, but we get on very well. I used to deliver phonebooks with him. I think he asked me to help because he was once friends with my older brother who has long left to work on the oil rigs off the west coast of Australia. I expect John enjoyed our untaxing chatter; it must have eased the boredom, and kept him somehow near to my brother.

A couple of times a week, I'd receive a text from him telling me to be at such-and-such a corner at such-and-such a time, and he'd roll up in his white Transit van and we'd drive on to some quiet suburb on the edge of Dublin. He'd hand me a high-vis vest, then slide back the door revealing a wall of phonebooks. We'd gather up ten at a time and run around like thieves dropping them, with slaps and claps, at doors and creaking gates. One evening – it had been raining hard – I wandered up to a red-brick house on the corner of a street in Rathfarnham: one of those Edwardian things that had been carved up into dark-windowed bedsits.

The front door was ajar. I heard a growl, then a bark, then the scrambling of paws on lino. I ran, and a black-and-white dog, whose breed I could not make out, lurched after me, chasing me down the driveway and out the front gate, me hurling books at it and it barking me further down the street, on and on, before it slowed, turned and trotted back up to the house.

I, hands on knees, heaved for breath until I noticed across the road a dozen schoolgoers, only a few years younger than me. They were staring. I tore off my high-vis vest and walked back to John's van, got in and told him nothing of the incident.

It was around then that Margaret and I finished. She left one day without a word. I came back to our apartment after work and I could tell in the stillness of the place that something was amiss. I chased to the bedroom, calling for her. I stood at the bedroom door unable to make out what was different until I realized that the only objects left in the room were mine. I pictured her picking our belongings apart, stalking around our room, separating and bagging her things, over and over until, with my eyes watering up, I took a mule-kick to the chest that launched me at great speed back out the door, crashing through the wall behind, through the neighbour's walls and through their neighbour's walls, on and on, crashing through walls, until I landed on my back out on the street, covered in dust, about half a block away. I haven't heard from her since. I feel like it's up to her to contact me, but she never has.

For months afterwards I collapsed into self-pity – drinking and smoking myself into a maudlin hoop each night – and I'd turn up surly and often late for John. He tried to lift my spirits, but we ended up getting less and less work done and he contacted me less often until he stopped texting altogether. Then, after almost a year, I eased off the drinking and smoking, returned to these small experiments of mine, got a job in this telesales centre and after a while I reconnected with John.

·

I count twenty-six petrol stations along this stretch of country road. As we drive I can see the hedges either side rustle in a breeze that seems to carry in it, gusts. After agreeing on how lost we are, John relents, pulls onto a station forecourt and steps into the shop. Moments later, a skinny aged man in navy overalls emerges with John and points across the road to the fields in the distance. On our way down I wanted to tell John about my latest experiment with the Oregon grape tree, but the way he looks at me of late, when I do update him on my extra-curricular projects, tells me that he ascribes to the uselessness of these experiments a certain childishness.

I lean forward and look out the front windscreen. The sky is massive down here. I have an urge to draw an infinitely large frame around it, then move everything one metre to my left.

John jumps in.

'Over there,' he says, pointing at the buckling horizon.

Ten minutes later we are a few miles off the main road. It's funny; in just ten minutes there is no one around and the land has emptied out – no cars, nothing – like we have travelled back in time to an Ireland from a hundred years ago. We approach a rusting steel gate leading into a field. Straggled herds of both brown and black-and-white cows mooch harmlessly before us. John produces two plastic bags from his pocket, bends over and ties them around his shoes. He runs a hand through his thick dark hair and looks to me, his broad and handsome face gormless with anticipation. I imagine he'd have been excitable company as a youngster.

'It looks smaller from here,' he says, leaping the gate, and we walk up the luscious hill to the stone tower at the summit. The cows, in their calm confusion, can't decide between dispersing or gathering around us.

The view from the hill is lovely: endless green fields edged out with dense rectilinear hedgerows. The breeze picks up and tosses our hair as we stand there gawping at the land. John fills and empties his lungs vigorously beside me, for almost a minute, to the point that I fear he might trigger an attack. He stops, pauses to say something significant, but – and this is why I love him – he doesn't. He just circumnavigates the tower that those British surveyors put up to orient us, all those years ago. John then slaps its surface, leans into it, as if he, the Samson of Smithfield, will topple it. I step to one side, pick up a stone and chuck it down the hill. It arcs, burrows, then disappears into the long grass like a terrified bird that has suddenly forgotten how to fly.

A farmer appears at the gate below and waves amiably up at us. He whistles the gate open and drives his old red roofless tractor in. The cows drift expectantly towards him. One piebald to the left of the herd breaks off and it walks with a strange determination through the fields leading west, on and on, until I lose sight of it.

The strange calmness of this place rests on me, and I take it easily. I picture John and myself as aimless black outlines on the summit. This place seems to invite at once purpose and total aimlessness, and I imagine, if I stayed here long enough, that once the feeling of purpose disappeared, all that would be left to do would be to leave, or sink to new depths of aimlessness, into a Good Friday of aimlessness.

The farmer clatters off to a distant field where he parades up and down spreading his gunk. The cows still follow. The engine throws revolutions up into the sky, thirstily, hoarsely over and over, breaking, louder, then receding, like waves on the shore of an inland lake on a quiet day.

John appears. 'The country air,' he says. 'There's something to it.'

We look out for some moments, then he shifts his weight in a way that might be called awkward.

'So I bumped into your Margaret there recently,' he says, finally. He coughs.

I turn to him. He coughs once more, but won't meet my gaze.

'She ask for me?' I say.

'No,' he says, 'I mean … No, she didn't. It's probably a few years for her now …'

We look at the land. I try to picture the centre point of the tower behind me.

'It seems she's pregnant anyway,' he says.

'Oh,' I say.

'With some lad from Cork,' he continues.

The bags at John's feet rustle as he shifts his weight once more. I look over my shoulder as the sun comes through; it draws a thick line on the ground, out from the base of the tower. Then the tower disappears leaving only its shadow. I turn back.

'Did you bring me all the way down here to tell me this?'

'I wasn't going to mention it,' he says. 'Then, in the van I thought I should, in case you ever saw her.'

I look at John and I can't think of anything to say and nor it seems can he, so we wander back down to his van and leave.

As I peer out at the evening light passing, my stomach aches at the thought of her. Then, I turn to John. He's focussing on the road.

'She's a bit young to be having kids though, no?' I say.

'Ah, not so young anymore, I wouldn't say,' he replies.

•

A few weeks later and I'm on the tram into town. It is early on a Saturday and the tram is peaceful and peopled only with a few shoppers and their quietly excited young children. I have brought the Oregon grape tree with me. I decided once I brought my experiment to a close that I ought to bring the plant back to the shop and see if they might take it and sell it to someone else, and perhaps even return to me a small percentage of what I spent.

I disembark and cross the tramlines and a few of the streets leading to the shopping centre, but I realize when I arrive that the plant shop opens later than usual on a Saturday. Beside it the health food store is opening up, admitting the first few customers – young men with long hair and tattoos down their forearms. I don't want to lumber this tree around with me all day so I decide instead to wait the half-hour or so before opening. I buy a takeaway coffee from the newsagents a few doors down and return to the bench. I flick through old text messages on my phone while listening to the thrum of the shopping centre coming to life.

Then, feeling a strange pull, I lift my head and I can see Margaret approaching the health food store. She is pushing a trolley along, looking at her phone. Her hair is still dark and long but she looks very large and she seems to have aged in her beautiful face. My chest tightens.

Something old then lifts into my throat. 'Margaret,' I croak.

'Margaret.'

She looks up from her phone, but her face alters in a way that saddens me. She looks away.

'Margaret,' I say once more, and I stand, pick up my Oregon grape tree and approach her.

Her green eyes soften, and I can't tell if it is because seeing me has made her sad, or if she has simply been reminded of someone she forgot about a long time ago.

'Why did you go?'

It just comes out. She looks back to her phone. It is buzzing – she silences it. She looks to the tree. Then, she looks to me.

'Your dreams, Lee, your dreams; they scared me,' she says, pushing strands of her hair from her earnest face, 'and I didn't want to tell you, because you always seemed so unworried when you woke, but when you slept, you scared me, Lee; you'd leap up, stand on the bed, crouch at its end, swinging your fist around at something that seemed terrible, and I thought you might eventually settle, but you never did, and I decided that if I wanted a baby, and I always wanted a baby, that I could never have a baby with a man that dreams like you.'

I can see in her face that she is serious.

'Why didn't you wake me?'

Her phone buzzes once again and she silences it once more. A family passes behind her. I can hear the checkout in the bright health shop ding.

'I didn't want,' she says, putting her phone away, 'whatever was in your dreams to come into your life. I thought if I just left, that it was the kindest thing I could do.'

I lean forward and place the Oregon grape tree into her trolley and tell her that I'd like her to have this small plant.

'It does well in the light,' I say.

'Oh,' she replies.

She looks at the tree, then she looks to me, then back to the tree once more, and I can tell that she will take it out of politeness but that it will almost certainly never see the inside of her home.

I remove it.

'It's hideous,' I say, 'isn't it? I only realized that when I saw it there in your trolley.'

'It is,' she smiles, and for a painful moment I can feel something of the easy humour that we once shared return; and when the pain passes something softens between us too.

'Can I touch it?' I ask, nodding towards her enormous belly.

And after a pause, she looks to me, and says, 'Of course.'

I put my hand onto her belly and I can feel a lovely warmth, but it is not a warmth that has anything to do with me, so I remove my hand.

'I hope you keep well,' I say, as she lifts her phone from her pocket, it lighting up and buzzing once more.

She leans forward and gives me a peck on the mouth; then she walks off, rolling her trolley towards the bustling health shop.

I place the Oregon grape tree between two benches and realize as I step back that it suits well these somewhat austere surrounds of echoing chrome and glass. I look again into the health shop, but Margaret is now typing something into her phone.

·

That evening, sitting on my settee – troubled by how Margaret described my sleep – I begin to wonder if I still behave in this way. I decide to devise an approach in the hope of learning more about it.

I think:

 1. Buy a camera and record my sleeping.

 2. Try to remember a dream.

 Then I decide that if I carry out option 1, what I see might frighten me away from carrying out option 2 and this might leave me stranded with – or worse, between – myselves. So I decide that option 2 is a more thoroughgoing approach and that it will yield deeper meaning and may even some day lead me back to confidently exploring option 1.

When I wake each morning the following week, I try to remember the dreams I've just left, but all I get in that strange dozing period of the day is a return to the sunny uplands of things that are not dreams, but mere aches made visual.

Then, one morning, a few days later, when lying in bed I decide to wait until I've had my first coffee and cigarette of the day before trying to recall my dream from the night before. So I rise, shower, and while I brew a coffee in my kitchen I smoke my morning cigarette. It is a Thursday and the glow of the beckoning weekend, I reckon, will surely help my remembrances sink more easily into the night before. I sit at my table and close my eyes and breathe and try to think back into what it was I dreamt. I can see nothing, and it occurs to me that perhaps the night before was a peaceful one and that there are no dreams troubling me enough to remember. I open my eyes to the kitchen clock ticking towards nine. I close my eyes once again and decide instead to remember back into my dreams through whatever sources of physical pain I most often wake to in the morning.

'Easy,' I say, 'my chest and my right fist.'

So I close my eyes and try to remember back into the place of my dreams through the dull throb that I feel each morning in my sternum and the heel of my right fist. It occurs to me that if my fist and my chest are painful in this dull way each morning, perhaps during the night I am striking my chest with my fist. So I visualize myself squatting like a gargoyle on my bed, in the dark and quiet, thudding away at my chest.

'Poor Margaret,' I utter.

I sit in my creaking kitchen chair for a while and think back through this image, but all it produces in me is an enlarging frame of malignancy, and as it gathers the quality of the malignancy becomes coarser and the frame falls away. I open my eyes before this gathering feeling becomes dense and sticky and I can feel my chest tighten and I realize I am merely sitting here in my own sunny kitchen now beating at my chest.

It is, all of a sudden, half-nine. I look around the kitchen to see if someone, while my eyes were closed, lifted the clock from the wall and wound the minute hand around by half an hour, or twelve-and-a-half hours, or twenty-four-and-a-half hours, or thirty-six …

I look to my fist in my lap, then I look at my still-steaming cup of black coffee. I look to the sunlight streaming in the small and mouldy kitchen windows and two things occur to me almost at once:

1. I don't really want to see what I see in my dreams.
and

2. Perhaps this state of affairs is not so bad and perhaps someday I will meet someone untroubled by my dreamtime activities, or perhaps even this person who might grow to love me might grow also to enjoy these shadowy erratic theatres I produce each night on our bed, and instead of being put out by it, perhaps this curious person will merely sit up in our

bed when, in the low part of the night, my jerking contortions begin, and this person, I hope, might simply choose to lie there in the dark looking on for a while, as I protect us from evil, and wonder, with mild amusement or perhaps even an aggregating boredom, as to wherefrom these small and ineffectual designs of my other self might come.

4

Midfield Dynamo

1.

My father was a one-woman-only kind of guy. It was as if, when he first met my mother, he had merely put his right hand out into a point in the universe, and she also happened to be there. The ease with which this union came about encouraged him to the point that he felt quite blessed. He then became quite blasé. And as I think about it now he was much more probably an unrepentant philanderer.

2.

My father, the year I was born, captained the local soccer club, a bunch of long-haired and moustachio'd outlaws. Their home games were played in a field just outside of town, a field that had been reclaimed from the bog some years previous. They had to finish all of their home fixtures that year by March because the owner of the field, a McCabe, wanted to have it ploughed by Easter.

That season the club played a cup quarter-final against a team from Dublin who arrived down one morning on a bus. All of the players got changed under the hedgerow that ran up the side of the pitch. Three members of my father's team turned up just before kickoff, smelling of beer. For an hour and a half twenty-two young men marauded in beautiful patterns up and down the pitch, and in between the moments of skill, vision and finesse, they kicked lumps out of each other. Then they shook hands, my father's team sympathizing with the team from Dublin. They all trudged from the field and my father's team bade farewell to the visiting team as they clambered, filthy, onto their bus, which was parked alongside the canal that wound its way under a stone bridge and through the black-and-green fields beyond. Then my father's team, every one of them, went home to their half-finished bungalows and had cold showers.

Later that night my father sat at his desk, lit the Superser gas heater, clicked on his desk lamp, cranked the head of it toward him, and neatly recounted all of the details of the game in his ledger, taking note of the result, exemplary performers and routes for improvement for the team both on and off the field.

3.

When I was seven or so my father built me a small timber goal. It was painted white, with a sewn-together patchwork of orange and yellow onion sacks as the net. I spent entire days kicking my ball into the goal, or saving balls kicked by my sisters and brother; and some nights I would sleep on my back underneath it, with my black-and-white leather football resting on my belly, slowly bobbing up and down with each breath. If the night turned chilly my father, I believe, would come out and drape a light blanket over me and the ball.

One roaring hot day a second or third cousin came to visit. He was an oaf of a lad. His first shot flew past my left ear and I could hear a seam between the onion bags rip open. I looked around and spied, through the hole in the netting, the ball lodged in one of the luminous leylandii bushes flanking the front drive. As my enormous jug-eared cousin crowed and celebrated around the lawn in front of me I thought two things:

1. I must get rid of this guy, or he will be the end of me.

2. My father shouldn't have stapled the bottom of the net to the base of the goal frame, he should have let the bottom of the net hang loose, so that there would be less strain on the netting seams under impact.

And to this day I am convinced that if it were not for this design fault, the goal would have had a longer life and would not have been discarded and so quickly left to rot, eventually to become a mere mound of white-paint-speckled pine-mulch and mesh at the bottom of our lawn.

4.

Most nights my father would go to the pub in town for a pint or two. Concerned for his safety, I'd lie awake until he returned. Then, as his car lights turned in from the road, around the bend in the driveway, and raked across my bedroom wall, I would allow myself to nod off. This was the case, unless my mother was angry, and on his return began shouting at him, to which he would mutter something apologetic and she would simply become angrier – then, I would sit up in my bed and listen keenly, hoping that everything would eventually settle.

One night, after the car lights were switched off and I heard the front door of the house close, my mother began shouting. She shouted for a long time, getting angrier and fiercer until I heard a bang and a tinny crumple, then silence. I ran down to the kitchen and my mother was sitting on the ground among the dozens of millionaire squares, baked earlier in the day, that had flown from the biscuit tin she had just hurled against the wall. I asked where my father was, and she looked up at me from the ground and said that he was long in bed asleep. Then she began to pick up the millionaire squares and eat them and I sat down beside her and ate too; then my brother and all of my sisters quietly appeared in the kitchen and we all sat on the ground and made small piles with the millionaire squares and ate the piles and then all of us kids passed out, not only because it was very late, but also because of the waves of sugar surging through our small bodies.

Next morning my father got up to find us bedraggled across the kitchen lino. He boiled the kettle, necked a glass of barely dissolved Disprin, looked out the window across the back drain and beyond at the cows mooching around the expanses of green fields, and he began grilling white sliced pan toast for us all, loaves of it, lathered in margarine, and flung four at a time, spinning down the length of the kitchen table to where we were all slowly beginning to gather.

5.

My father once told me about the night he turned up half-cut at a dance. He was fourteen or so, and the dance was taking place in the library hall at the top end of town.

He caught the eye of a girl that was new to the scene. She was a few years older than him but they started to chat. Then they took a walk out of the library hall and back down the town, in behind a garage, where they climbed into the two front seats of a smashed-up car and began to kiss and cuddle, until my father, enlivened, dropped his hand, only to find that the girl had a leg that was made of wood.

She became embarrassed at his surprise.

They sat apart for a while and it began to rain outside. He told me they could hear the drops bounce on the roof of the car, on the badly creased bonnet, on the boot, the folded rusting side panels of the car doors, the cracked side windows and the front and back windscreens. He told me he couldn't think why those details had stuck. They promised to meet in the car every night for the rest of her holidays.

And for the next four nights my father and this girl met up in this wreck and kissed and fondled with fervour and love.

6.

My father's parents owned a dance hall in the middle of the town. It was the only one of its kind in this part of the county. When my father was very young he used to watch the loving crowds jive and spin from between the shapely balusters on the upstairs landing. By the time he was six he began offering jiving classes to those he deemed in need of them. His instructions were clear, earnest, roomy, inexpensive and fell on attentive ears.

By the time he was seven, my father had tired of the commitment to these ever-growing weekly classes, so he passed the responsibility for them on to a student who had excelled over the course of the year – he a retired dairy farmer from north Longford whose life suddenly brimmed with purpose.

7.

When the dance hall that my father's parents owned closed down, they opened a cinema in town. And when everyone in the town and the immediate hinterland had seen the current release, my father was sent out in the family car with the projector and reels to other outlying village and parochial halls.

In these small darkened halls, clusters of families from the surrounding townlands would convene. Afterward, driving home through the dark and winding roads, my father would look on at the illuminated ribbon of hedge-lined tarmac appearing continuously before him only for it to disappear almost immediately again beneath and out behind him to rejoin the darkness from which it had come.

One wet and very windy night when he eventually got back to the shadows of his parents' house, he walked in on his father at the end of the downstairs hallway sitting on the hall seat and smoking – the tip of his cigarette glowing like a distant carbide-battery lamp being carried through the lowland fogs away from a steaming hedgerow car wreck.

8.

When my father drove us – all of my sisters, my brother and I – into town for our Saturday-night bag of chips, he would often draw our attention to the distant streetlights of the town and point out how, if you joined the dots, it resembled a large amber arrow pointing diagonally downward from the sky to the earth. He reasoned that the point of the arrow was directed toward the part of the town where his parents' house would have stood, it being on the bend of the street. As we drove closer to town, the arrow slowly dissolved around us until we became part of its electric umber, sitting outside the chip shop in the back of his car waiting for our warm packets of vinegar-sodden chips.

On the way home we were too busy eating to bother looking out the rear window of the car to see the arrow re-forming in the sky behind us.

There is the town before my father, and then there is my father's town – the one he built for ten years. My father's town was built into and around the old one. It was made up of new houses, apartments, industrial units, garages, shops; and such was the way these developments sprawled outward and embalmed the old town that, if you were now to drive in to the town, the arrow that once hovered in the sky above it has transformed into an amorphous cluster of amber, yellow, red and orange pixels.

9.

For a few years my father's father worked as the clerk of works in the Midlands division of the Rural Electrification Scheme. One bright evening in late summer he and my father took a trip out to an elderly lady in a small village fifteen miles from town. She had written to say that she wanted to see my grandfather.

She greeted them at the door and smiled at my father – a curious sort – who was peering up at the white electrical wires running across the underside of the eaves of her thatched cottage, taking note of how the cable was fastened to the soffit at regular intervals with white plastic hoops. My grandfather apologized for not getting out sooner, and this elderly lady said it was fine, and that they should come in for a cup of tea.

They sat in front of the fire and the woman pottered around in the half-darkness of her two-roomed house and eventually produced three white and sky-blue-rimmed cups of tea. She sat and talked at length to my grandfather about her husband, who had passed away in early spring. She spoke quietly about how lonely she felt and how she missed him, and eventually my father nodded to sleep, the drained teacup slumping incrementally from his lap until it finally slipped and dangled by its handle from his curled index finger. He slept through her story and was roused only when his father nudged him that they were to leave. When they emerged from the low front door of the house it was as if the evening had somehow become brighter and the air had become lighter too, so light that my father felt that if he had wanted he could have taken flight up over the house, trees and fields, beyond the moon and stars and out into the universe, beyond the systems, beyond the dark, beyond everything, until he disappeared forever. My grandfather turned to say goodbye to the woman, but she asked them to wait a moment because she had something for him. When she returned she placed a large one-hundred-watt glass bulb into my father's hands. She said that she had never wanted the electricity in the first place and now never uses it, and as she grasped her pink crocheted cardigan about her slim chest and waist, she said, this bulb has been putting my fire out and making my house feel small at night, and I am afraid that the thatch will take flame from it too.

My grandfather, who had heard these poorly reasoned arguments a thousand times before and knew every line and official response to counter them, took the bulb out of my father's hands and said to this woman standing at her low door: thank you for the tea, and it was lovely to see you in any case, and perhaps I will see you again the next time we are doing work in this part of the county, and if you ever change your mind, there is no problem at all getting this bulb back, because I will keep it safe for you.

10.

My father's father opened a bookie's in a long-disused butcher shop in the middle of town, the weekend before an FA Cup Final. Going against his son's calculations, my grandfather misjudged the odds on the races in Leopardstown that Sunday too, and by the following Wednesday he had to close down because he was unable to pay the next week's rent.

My father refused to help him take down the signage or empty the ashtrays that were overflowing and spilling from the counters onto the many crumpled chits and betting slips on the floor. So my grandfather swept the entire property down himself, cleaned the windows, pulled the blinds and left through the front door, where he stood for a moment and looked up and down the broad main street of the town to see that it was empty of people and completely still.

8

Prosinečki

I can hear the crowd above me erupt again, but this time with far more heat than the roar that greeted the second-half whistle not minutes ago. Shudders pass down through the walls of the changing room as the mass of people overhead leap once more to their feet. The shudders dispel. My teammates told me, with the rain that fell in the first half, that the pitch will take a stud. The changing room is empty now. It smells of oranges, sweat and muscle rub. I pull on my studs and begin to lace them up.

Our stadium is an old thing in the middle of northern England, surrounded by long-stilled steel and iron works and a network of congealing canals. I often think the fans come here just to be among the decaying trusses that shelter our deep single-tiered stands. Old men and women with their grandchildren usually people the seats, along with pockets of harmless, drunk and overweight men on cheap season-tickets who obsess over transfers to and from the club. Tonight, like at every home game, these men gather in a sprawling sky-blue-and-white horde across the South Stand. This club was never great – but it seems to exist now only out of the ghost of some habit.

Shoving and shouting flares up from the end of the corridor that leads out onto the pitch. I look up for a moment; then, I return to lacing up my boots.

The physio has just left, having injected two painkillers into either side of my now gently bloating knee. Our manager, Marco, a tall bellying Londoner, told me during the break in play that I'd be getting some time near the end of the game. I've been here six years, but for the last three I have been more injured than not. Yet the supporters love me, their limited but committed midfielder; I play as they would play. This knee, now stiff with painkillers, is permanently destroyed. It mocks this puerile comeback of mine in a mid-table game on this wet pointless night in late March. It's not that I need the money – I've been careful over the years, but if I can get another contract at even half of my current wage I'll be able to buy a fine two-bed apartment in town, one I've had my eye on for a while now, one I can rent out and make a few extra bob off after I retire.

The tumult at the end of the hallway has died down and I can hear the purposeful clink of studs on concrete. Collins, our midfielder, boots the door open. He's laughing ruefully.

His gaunt face is bloody, a cut above the eye, and his shirt is torn at the neck. He pushes his shining dark hair off his face.

'Gaffer wants you,' he says as he sits, panting for breath, 'kicked off a bit out there.'

'You off? Cooper?'

'I had to … He won't do that again.'

'Straight swap?' I say, standing and stretching out my knee.

'Into the middle with Nat. Fat fucker's having a mare,' he says, peeling a boot off.

'Did Cooper get up?' I ask.

'Yea,' says Collins, as I leave him sitting on the bench, pulling off his shirt and steadying his breath.

He'll soon be showered and back out to watch the remaining ten of us struggle. I can hear the drums, and the crowd's voice gathering above me as I stride down the corridor towards the opening of light.

Marco appears at the entrance, gesturing me towards him. He has his notebook folded open in his hand. As I step from the tunnel, he puts his arm around my shoulders and walks me to the sideline. The crowd in the stand behind us roar. I unzip and throw aside my tracksuit top.

'Just fill in for Col. Stay behind the ball. Get Nat up the pitch,' he shouts into my ear, while pointing at a page in his notebook, it filled with lines, arrows and numbers.

The linesman checks my boots and hands, and I step on. The crowd begins to call my name as I jog to the centre circle. Nat, a blond lad from Lincoln, puts out his hand as

I approach, and as I touch it I lean in and say, 'I'll sit, you kick on.'

He nods.

Their centre-forward, this lanky and sly operator, Cooper, who is top scorer in our division and on his way up the leagues to a more prestigious club, walks over to say something; he comes in close and tries to stud my foot. I step back, shake my head impatiently, as if he were a young child, and tell him to fuck off. I jog to the edge of the circle.

We all turn as their goalkeeper restarts play, hoofing a goal kick up towards the centre-right of the pitch. We jostle to challenge, and the sound and colours around me fall away, and in flows, in their stead, dull pain.

·

The ball bounces loose in the middle of the park. I hook it over my shoulder, hoping it will land just inside their box because for the last twenty minutes their centre-halves have been pushing up the pitch and our right-winger, an earnest young man on loan here, has been making diagonal runs across their defence. But the older centre-half, Thirlwell, a guy I played with years before, sees immediately what I was trying to do. He backtracks and hacks my pass over our heads, returning it down the field. The ball, a sphere of ivory in the night sky, gets lost in the floodlights, re-appears, bounces; and our keeper, Arterberry, comes out to catch, but he is upended by this Cooper.

Arterberry is out cold. That frightening dead-man inertia came over his body when he landed and the ball just rolled off his stomach. Our medics rush to him. I jog towards the sideline, catch my breath and loosen out my knee. The water I skoosh into my mouth splatters the back of my throat. I pour some onto my face and peer around at the crowd of seven thousand or so. The few hundred of rowdy travelling support are tucked away up in the North Stand, but the whole place has gone utterly quiet. Everyone is fixated on Arterberry splayed on the ground amid plumes of vapour and hunkering medics. The rain, gently falling now, spins in thin films down out of the black above me, over the edges of the roofs of the stands and through the rectangle of floodlights that frames the sky. My breathing has modulated but my heart is thumping coarsely. Our home-supporters' voices come up as Arterberry gets to his feet. They are chanting one of the club's old classics: something about being on a beach in Bari. It's a sort of over-unionized chorus that has begun, of late, to sound like a lament.

I played well here in the first two seasons, scoring double figures and keeping us in the middle of the league. Then I hurt my knee during pre-season – a torn tendon, a repeat of one I picked up when I was twenty-three and on trial at a club in the top division.

That first knee injury came just days before I secured a contract there. When I left, emptied out, the club recommended a knee-specialist in Munich, to whom I went for ten months, over and back, with no club and no wage and diminishing savings. I regularly bumped into another young midfielder there. A German guy called Uwe, a polite slight muscular chap who played in the second division for an old East-German club outside of Berlin. We chatted often about swimming and gym work and the top German tier, and we went for lunch on occasion. Once my knee repaired he convinced me to travel up to his club, and with no other offers on my plate I decided to trial. I got fit again, became very strong and played well, so they gave me a two-season contract. They had a large following of what looked like mostly neo-Nazis to me, but they had a beautiful stadium, in the middle of a vast forest that shoehorned around a deep and peaceful lake.

I was in my mid-twenties then and after eight months finding my rhythm I became as rapid and healthy as I have ever been. I never really drank and almost none of these Germans did either. Some of them smoked and a Turkish player, Umit, would sometimes take me to his parents' café in Wedding on the west side of Berlin where we'd puff happily for hours on a shisha. Other than that I spent my afternoons after training visiting erotic massage parlours in town – local, Thai, Latvian – then I'd drive back out to my spacious apartment, prepare dinner, read and sleep. Being injured and being a good professional over the years taught me how to suppress my energy between games and to live as a lesser god. I soon learned some football German and began dating a local girl called Stefanie, but during the winter break in my second season, while on holiday with her in Kos, I slipped on the tiling beside the hotel swimming pool and ruptured a ligament that neighboured the one I'd torn before. I didn't play again for a year. I blamed Stefanie and stopped seeing her. I focussed furiously on getting well again, but what disappointed me most was that it happened at a time when I was dictating games, when my circle of influence around the team was widening and becoming more intense. My personality was extending through the field of play, sometimes into the opposition's shape, and my opponents couldn't dismantle it, no matter how hard they hit me. My Englishness was exotic there, and my range of passing broadened in that forest in Brandenburg, short unlikely passes and long cross-field pings, switching play emphatically. I cast out nets of influence over the pitch that allowed my inner-city Leeds swagger to appear, and when it did – a nutmeg, a no-look pass – it was cheered brutally by the loving crowd. I'd wave to them at the end of games and they'd howl back at me. I scored eight times during the first half of that season, but more than anything else, my footballing intellect was developing at a great rate. I wasn't just picking out passes before the ball came to me, I could see the pass after that as well; I was three vectors ahead of the fluxing present, becoming a roving pivot between our defence and attack. I then began to intuit when the opposition started reading me and would mix my play up between: passing, or keeping the ball, or turning on it, or holding. I was at once far above and deep within the eddies of play – in short, at this lesser but accomplished level of football, I was approaching some genius.

Arterberry has to sit back onto the grass, while a medic takes hold of his head. The crowd, who have been restless all night, have settled down again. Only the away fans, with their interminable clanging cow bell, keep singing. They sound like a country choir on a small-town pier, but one detaching from the mainland and floating out to sea. I stretch out my knee and my hip as I return to the centre circle. Nat jogs over, badly out of breath. He is a handsome lad, with more talent than discipline, and will most likely balloon when he retires. He's been hectoring our right-back for the whole night. 'The Child,' he calls him.

Nat stands beside me, panting. He puts a finger to his nostril and clears the other. He spits, makes to move away; then, he leans back and says, 'The Child's fucking killing me.'

'He's not going to feet is he,' I say, as I step past him. 'What's he so nervous about?'

Nat jogs away to approach the opposition's other centre-back, Miller, who has walked up to talk to his midfielders. Miller, a tall dark-haired man, looks around at Nat and they break into a smile. I think they were on an England underage squad once. Nat jogs off again, now towards the medics and the stricken Arterberry. It's all a show, but the crowd still croons his name. He hates Arterberry and Arterberry hates him. Nat lobbed him during shooting practice on Arterberry's first day at the club – 'You just don't do that, mate,' he called plaintively to Nat, who jogged away laughing, 'You do if you can mate, y'do if you can.'

I stretch my knee out again, and look to the side of the dugout. The crowd's voice falls away behind. Collins is taking a seat, dressed in his blue tracksuit, his hair gelled back and his right eye stitched up, but the socket is blackening. He turns to talk to a steward. Marco, his cupped hand by his mouth, is shouting something to Nat. Arterberry standing now in front of our medic, a tall white-haired Scottish woman in her late fifties. She is holding her index finger up in front of Arterberry's eyes, moving it over and back. Nat nods to Marco, gives him the thumbs-up and jogs back towards me. The home crowd come back into voice – it's a chant aimed at goading the away supporters into response. The melody drifts across the pitch as mist rolls in over the floodlights. The away fans sing back.

There was a time, early in my career, when before each game I'd watch the grainy videos I'd collected since my teens of my favourite player, the tall blond Croatian, Robert Prosinečki. I'd lie on my bed, close my eyes and re-visualize his movement: when he lifted his head, when he controlled the ball, rolling it under his foot, the way he used his body to shield himself and how he span away from bewildered defenders at the least likely moment. I analyzed him when he was young and turning out for Red Star Belgrade, then kings of the soon-to-crumble Yugoslavian leagues. I modelled my play, as a young man, on the brio I detected from him.

One night, two weeks before I snapped my ligament in Kos, we were playing a team from Cologne. It was midway through the second half of a tight nasty game when I received a pass that had been zipped at me from our left-back. I was on the midway line, with my back to goal, and as the ball sped to me through the sleet I feigned right and clipped the ball with the inside of my foot, back across my body and past my left knee. Then, feeling the entire earth rushing over my right shoulder, I span left, and the pitch, the stadium, the lights, the forest cleaved open before me. The crowd's voice surged as I pushed the ball towards the developing frames of possibility. Both of their fullbacks were way beyond our wingers. One of their centre-halves was drawn left while the other advanced on me – a tall ageing Pole, Nowak. I ought to have shown him more respect, but I was young and full and I knew my midfield partner, Uwe, would be running hard in a shallow arc behind me, so I made eyes left and shaped to pass but instead slowed, leaned back and scooped the ball high and right. And as the ball arced insolently over poor steadfast Nowak, Uwe sped past me and advanced irrevocably beyond him. Uwe took the ball down with his instep, looked at the keeper chasing out and rolled it to his left. The crowd bellowed. Nowak slumped on the edge of the box, head down, but Uwe was off, swinging his shirt in the air, sprinting to the corner flag. The ultras poured down savagely through the stand. Our left-back jumped onto my shoulders and roared, hurling his fist in the sleet-filled air. He landed beside me and we tore off towards Uwe and the rest of the players. I leapt onto the huddle and bared my teeth at the corner of broiling white men, and hollered banal non-words into them all. As I jogged back to the centre circle I thought the same thoughts I always thought when I was playing well in Brandenburg: that I could run like this forever, that there is no limit to my Cartesian aptitude, that I am a conqueror here, that I am showing my football-culture to be finer and that I am ready to return and present myself again in England, the only place where any of this has worth, or makes proper sense to me; it is the only place where the admiration is appropriate, and, as my heart pounded and I tracked down their kickoff, I thought, it is the only admiration that will last satisfyingly beyond my career where I might be recognized for my deeds as an ageing, broad-shouldered and bronzed ex-pro in my forties and fifties and sixties, entering a café, perhaps, in some quiet West-Midlands town, or a restaurant in Newcastle, or the clubhouse of a cricket club on a quiet Tuesday afternoon in a suburb in York.

Arterberry has had to lie down again. They are calling the stretcher from the sidelines and an ambulance pulls up at the mouth of the tunnel of the East Stand. Our substitute keeper, Wilson, a young Northern Irishman, is warming up with a heartless vigour. I wonder how many times he has wished Arterberry dead. Along the sideline the goalkeeping coach dropkicks shots at Wilson, who catches with a conspicuous mixture of method and what looks like instinct. He will never be a great keeper, he is too in love with technique, but he will earn well and convince many. I imagine, when he is much older, should fortune offer him a moment of lucidity, he will look back on his sporting life as a mechanical insult to his position. He runs onto the pitch fisting his gloves as Arterberry is carried off. Arterberry, prone in the stretcher, lifts his arm to the crowd, who cheer as if he were a miner being lifted from a blast. The referee gives a drop-ball, which Cooper steps up to and hoofs disdainfully into the crowd behind our goal; and they jeer. Cooper jogs, then strides back up the pitch and turns for the kick-out, and as the players gather around the centre circle, like steaming cattle awaiting feed, he looks over his shoulder, smirks and makes a what-can-you-do? type shrug at me. If I was younger I'd aim to nail him before the end of the game, but there's too much at stake, and though the crowd may bay their approval, Marco would see through it and if I get a red card he'll strike me from his reckoning for the three games I'm banned for and then, most likely, for the rest of season too.

I look to the seats above our dugout and spy an ancient Irish gentleman, Lawrence, who has not been to the ground for some time. He used to be a coach at my old schoolboy club. He was a goalkeeper and had large beautiful hands and white slicked-back hair. After training one day – I was four-teen then and Leeds United had invited me to their academy for the summer – I stayed behind to practise with one of the other boys, Graham, who was as sweet a footballer as I've ever seen, but never came to anything. As we walked back to the clubhouse to change, Lawrence appeared and asked me to walk with him.

It was raining heavily as we strode over and back along the centre line of the pitch for almost an hour, him advising me about going to Leeds at this age, and the sort of lads I'd be up against and how many people fail there – but it is how you take the failure, he said, and what you learn from it that contributes to you as a footballer. As your body and mind develop, he continued, particularly in your central position, and if you are wise and lucky, you will get a sweet spot in your career when your body can carry your developing mind, and your mind will then push the body beyond what you thought possible, creating new positions, new patterns, new time, he said, with rain pouring down his face, and you will feel this moment for a brief period in your life, son, and you must remain limber enough to feel it, to act and expand on it ... This sweet spot, he continued, will happen during a game when the arcs of adrenaline, exhaustion, familiarity, daring and a recent history of good physical condition coincide, and you must treat that moment, or these moments, with a cavalier preciousness, and make them your own by making them memorable for those looking on, and if you can do this, son, even once, truly, then, he said, you will have achieved something as a footballer.

He is sitting in the stand under a sky-blue-and-white hat. He looks old and cold. My stomach voids. My knee trembles. I think how wrong he was. I think too how foolish I have been, for believing for years in that crap and for believing too that that moment against the team from Cologne was the high point of my vocation, when in fact, I realize, jogging across the centre circle of the pitch, barking orders at our left-winger, that it was my lowest point ... Throughout my career I'd been so focussed on moments in games where the aesthetic effect took precedence over the pragmatic decision, that I'd failed to realize through watching Prosinečki for all of those hours, that it is the pragmatic that serves the aesthetic – that it is only from the core of good service that any beauty can bloom. If I'd analyzed Prosinečki properly, I'd have seen that his decisions were always at the service of what was necessary as he faced the manifold problems emerging before him on the pitch. Even though the most beautiful pass might be available to him during a game, he always chose the most effective, the one few footballers ever see – or do see, but are too vain to take – playing in clichés of what is great, hitting entertaining passes, passes that are similes without sentences. But Prosinečki, as if playing for no crowd, always made the most moral decision on the ball. He solved the problems on the pitch in a way that developed the moment back upon itself, but with one small alteration that split the game open, and each alteration he made was balanced and fair, and furthered an abundance that each game was already germinating, an abundance that did not require an opponent to be humiliated, an appropriate abundance that I and everyone else who speaks of him has misinterpreted as flair.

This, and, what I'd perceived as the high point of my career are just two shades of the same ugly daub, and I realize my very worst crime was what I thought was my very greatest moment, the one those supporters in that small club near Berlin will remember me for forever. I would do well to go back and apologize to Nowak and to everyone who witnessed it, and to disown everything in my life that led to it, and beyond it, to now; but, there is nothing I can do, and no way for me to repent. I am a spent age-thickened footballer mooching around a large circle with a line through it, in the middle of a city I care little for.

Wilson is shaping to boot the goal-kick up the pitch, but he spies The Child dropping deep to take it off him. He rolls the ball out to him, and because Arterberry didn't try this during the game our opposition is out of shape to receive our attack. The Child turns out with the ball, raises his head, and with a morphinic excitement I spy a gap opening towards the right side of their box. I take off, and The Child floats a cultured back-spinning pass up the channel and as I sprint I can see Nat come across to meet it. His shoulders arch, his neck muscles slacken and he glances the pass off the top of his head. The ball loops into my bending path and skims out in front of me, and I sense my opponent behind as I chase towards where the ball will bounce again, and skid and roll, and I feel like I am clear and free. A silence comes over me as I take a touch, but the touch is terrible, and has put me too wide and the ball is gone too long and my right leg has been clipped and I should really go to ground, and I can hear the crowd scream for me to do so, as if nothing would make them happier. But to my left I glimpse our striker powering alone into the box, and if I can dink the ball across to him he will surely score. I know too, that if I fall I will be reconnected with my past, so I straighten, and my legs out of dumb momentum begin to gather and re-coordinate beneath me and I realize that if I propel myself and stretch for this disappearing ball and dink it back across the box, that somehow I will have done enough. I lunge, feet first, and scissor my right foot desperately at the base of the ball. As I connect and slide over the line, I can see the ball spinning handsomely back up and away from me, towards a space in front of our striker, whose eyes and mouth have widened, his arms have spread, his feet have skipped, his knees are bent and he lifts himself diagonally up to where my cross is going. The ball slows into its languid arc, and as his body coils and his eyes wince shut, bringing him into the great pre-impact dark that every footballer knows, I gasp deeply, once more, at the impotent, incidental and unforgiveable beauty of it all.

11

Half Bird Half Bear

One day, when I was fifteen or so, my grand-uncle-in-law, Wojciech, and I were sitting outside the main train station in Dresden waiting for a bus to take me back to the airport in Berlin. From there I would fly on home to Dublin. The week before, we had buried his wife, my grand-aunt, Bernadette, in a cemetery in the suburbs of Wrocław. It was the Easter holidays and my parents thought it would be a good idea for me to stay on for a few days after the funeral and keep Wojciech company.

The afternoon was bright and breezy. People were crossing over and back in front of us as we sat on the bench. The footpath was narrow, so there was much tutting and fussing as people negotiated the station's entrance. Wojciech and I were lost again in saying nothing to each other and we didn't notice that my bags were causing the obstruction. A frail bespectacled old man in a white button-up shirt – dotted with prints of hot-air balloons, conifer trees, rucksacks, wolves, bi-planes – sidled over and he, assuming that I was not from here, said, in accented English, 'Your bags are causing disruption, sirs. May I move them?'

Then, without waiting for our reply, he lifted my shoulder bag and rucksack to one side. Then, he trotted off.

Wojciech and I sat uncomfortably for almost a minute, until he turned to me and said, 'You know, this busybody has implied that we are inconsiderate.'

I did not reply. I could not grasp Wojciech's sense of grievance, nor could I ignore it. It was not for the first time that week I fell short of the pitch of his world. I looked at my watch. The bus would be along in five minutes. Wojciech and I prepared to bid farewell to each other.

I had grown fond of him. During the day he was kind, patient and at times lively company; but it was our night-time encounters in the hallway of his small apartment that I will never forget. He sleepwalked each night, quietly raving to himself, then calling out scarily into the dark, until I led him back to bed.

The sun slid behind a cloud, then reappeared, warming our faces. A bus accelerated away leaving a grey cloud of exhaust that uncoupled from itself, in spirals, before being carried away by the breeze.

'You know, I once had two uncles, fine tall men – twins!' Wojciech said. 'They were from Ukraine. Sergei was a geologist and Eugene an actuarist. They were both clever and were well-respected men too. Before the War they worked as advisors at a quarry near my hometown on the Polish side of the border and they often visited us. I was a young boy then, but I remember my mother, who was their older sister, at first remarked on how graceful she thought my two uncles were, bringing their education and refinement in among us parochial people. After they'd leave though, and this made me laugh, she always said she preferred dark-haired Sergei. He was the younger brother by almost three days. My mother would say that he had an easy grace – whereas she called Eugene 'conspicuously graceful' – and that he was often a fraction over-thankful and over-attentive in our house, and these small performances of his, over the course of his visit, eventually got right up her nose.'

I looked at Wojciech's creased hands opening and folding and turning in among themselves as he spoke. Then he rested them in his lap – like two small animals in love.

'Apparently Sergei was a great shot with the rifle,' he continued, 'and when he was younger he hunted squirrels. He would go to the markets in his village and the villages nearby, each Saturday, and sell squirrel fur. He told me once that the only way to shoot a squirrel was through the eye, otherwise the pelt would be singed and ripped and ruined. Then, Eugene and Sergei were called up to the army and during the War Eugene was killed when the Germans advanced east, and, as they were thrust back west, Sergei fronted up one column of this counter-attack. He received a Red Star medal for blowing up a lone Panzer not far from here. But he did not ever recover from losing his brother and he didn't visit us again.'

I wondered at the time where Wojciech's memory was going. I looked to him, his hands trembling.

'Sergei died of hypothermia two winters later. He was found one morning curled up in the snow, in the middle of a field outside of his village, after drinking for a week. He'd pawned his medal for vodka. Many months after the funeral, my mother learned of what happened, so she travelled to his village to buy the medal back, but the broker had already sold it to a local timber merchant whose asking price, when my mother tracked him down, was far too much. She returned home empty-handed.'

Later that evening, on my flight back to Ireland – as the plane arced over a white disintegrating trail below – I pictured this Sergei as a boy of my age, crouching through the edge of a great forest full of gigantic autumnal trees, slowly turning his rifle over in his hands, hunting his squirrels. I thought for the first time in the aeroplane, and still do think, what a strange word squirrel is, with that 'ir' pushing up through the middle of it, and how strangely Wojciech, who passed on less than a year later, pronounced the word too, almost as if he ignored that 'ir'.

'Screwil,' he said.

And when he first uttered this word I'd no idea what he was talking about until he acted out the movements of a squirrel sitting on a branch eating a nut. I looked out the window of the plane as the land passed peacefully below me and I rolled the word around in my mouth; then I wrote it down on the back of my ticket. I tried to imagine all of the squirrels Sergei must have killed and skinned and whose fur he sold. And it's only now I think about the ones he missed, with a distant clatter and whizz. And I can see at last a squirrel fleeing from the end of a bobbing branch. And in the sylvan quiet of this moment, I imagine this squirrel as a mere kernel of panic imploding, then opening, imploding, then opening … it heaving and floating forever there, in the damp forest air – half bird, half bear.

UP FRONT

Forty-eight Pots of Honey

Three things wake me each morning. First is an alarm clock belonging to my upstairs neighbour who works as a bin collector for the local council; the second is the swarms of airplanes that thrust east out over the city, one after another, like giant untethered circular saws splitting the sky over and over, until it is, I imagine, a smithereened tectonic of swirling blue rhombuses; the third thing that wakes me is Christian, my third child out of four. His name is pronounced *Kris-tee-ann*, or so my wife, Bettina, insisted the day he was birthed in the back seat of a friend's car I'd borrowed, because I cannot afford my own. Bettina and I were on a motorway lay-by on the way to the hospital after her waters broke; '*Kris-tee-ann!*' she bellowed as I called an ambulance, but before it arrived Christian had already appeared and was beginning his first gentle mewlings. Bettina, though, was cold, exhausted, her thighs bloody, and she was thirsty and anxious. I was beside myself with worry. After the ambulance doors closed and it calmly drove off with her and Christian inside, I went home, made a hot chocolate and rang our neighbour to say I would be over presently for the two older kids, Horst and David. I then lit our gas fire and lay on the couch, and as the heat began touching my face and my arms I bolted to the kitchen of our tiny apartment and threw up in the sink and thought, with my stomach spasming horribly, how Christian and I already had a particular connection, seeing as I delivered him, or at least helped to, or at least I saw him in his entirety first – the godless gestalt of that moment. In any case, the third thing that wakes me in the morning is small red-headed Christian, now almost six years old, quietly climbing into bed beside my beautiful Bettina and I.

Our youngest, Karl, has started kindergarten so Bettina has once more returned to her work as a legal aide. She was a lawyer when I first met her, but once we had our eldest, Horst, she began working part-time as a legal aide for a firm of lawyers on the third floor of a terraced building three cobbled streets away from our apartment. I work odd jobs. My last was in a market selling bread for my local bakery. I'd stand for hours among the large-boned folk from the hinterlands of the city and sell dark-seeded breads wrapped in newspaper. Over the course of the winter, I'd become increasingly miserable and resolve to get a job indoors. Every winter it snows here for months until the whole place ought to come to a standstill, but the city struggles on inventively through its yard-upon-yard-thick fields of snow, its citizens like long-distance swimmers near a coastline with its waters covered in lard and felt and hare hides. The weather in spring, however, is astonishing; but the summer I find too hot, and in the park people lie around naked in the long grass all day, shining limbs bent skyward like small animals swaying drunkenly in the arid shimmer; the autumn then is colourful and astonishing too; and the winter, et cetera ...

When I am between jobs I try to write. I get a week or two every now and then and I go to a café near my house. The café is inexpensive, pleasant and quiet; lacquered-steel-and-unstained-timber furniture, and little ornamentation – no cushions, no music. No children are admitted, no parents with buggies, no fathers with infants swaddled, no women with toddlers; no people that might harass the quiet. The café owner, Sebastian, is forthcoming and firm when he explains to people with children why they cannot enter; and they hate him. He speaks in a pedantic way but with a wobbly syntax and sometimes looking on at him speaking I realize that his words are things that suppress a rampant if unwieldy death drive. He tells these people that he has three children of his own, but there need to be some places for quiet in this city, some places where the expectation of quiet is possible, and his café is one. During my visits the café is often empty for hours, me at a table under the window of the front section, scribbling or typing, and he in the back cooking or rolling a cigarette. He smokes these cigarettes every twenty minutes or so. I think he does this to break the frustration of knowing, because he has made his café so quiet, that he will have to throw most and sometimes all of this food out. And because I am not intrusive company he often appears beside me and wordlessly leaves a saucer of food on the table with a fish fork wrapped in a small pastel-green serviette. As he walks away I utter a subtle, 'Thank you, Sebastian.'

Today is tremendously peaceful. It is snowing outside. The massive window of the café frames the descending flakes, each one the still centre of innumerable falling universes. I am writing about a man listening with growing disinterest to his brother who is describing a dream he had that morning where he saw his feet over the edge of his bed but realized that he could not put on his socks, and not because he was paralyzed, but because he had left his body and was entering his first reverse-moments of death. But because he had been happy in his life and wanted to go through with it, and to begin that day by putting on his socks, this brother felt an unspeakable disappointment at being dead, which amassed into a feeling of unendurable neutrality that almost as soon as it appeared, it sluiced itself, from its core, into a stark feeling of motherlessness. This brother then realized he could not weep, and this motherlessness, the aloneness of being aware, for a moment, of his endless death began to gather and mound and surge into the sorts of feelings he had no words for, even in his dreams, and with that he woke and was incrementally swathed in three types of relief ...

But I am unable to write these brothers out of this scene, or imagine what these species of relief might feel like or how they might best be described, and anyway, Sebastian has come from the kitchen and has taken a seat on the bench in front of me and asks, as he rolls a cigarette, 'Peter. Sorry to intrude on your writing, but are you able to drive?'

I smile, angle my notebook and write across the page, 'I can drive, Sebastian; I don't like to, but I can.'

'I have a favour,' he replies. 'Could you collect some honey for me, from my producer, Mrs Berg? She is old and lives forty miles north of here. I forgot that she leaves tomorrow morning for two months in Trieste, and I need the honey because I am all out. I'm uncomfortable asking because you seem to be working, but could you drive out and collect it?' he continues, licking the glue of his cigarette paper. 'I will pay you fifty euros for just two hours driving. You can use my camper van; it is full of diesel and is sturdy.'

I look out the window silently.

'Please,' he says. 'I have customers expecting … I will throw you in a pot for nothing. Now what do you think?!'

I am in the van easing out of the city limits. The motorway has narrowed to a single-lane carriageway and the snow has not stopped. There was a small orange gritter speeding ahead of me earlier, but it now passes me on the way back, having turned, I presume, at the state border. The sides of the road are heaped in black-and-white snow and it is getting dark. I despair at this van; it is cold, sluggish and rear-wheel-drive, and whenever I meet an incline of any sort the front wheels veer around the place and at times I have no control at all. Sebastian told me that Mrs Berg lives two miles off exit 16 of this road that goes north to a small riverless city from where Sebastian's first wife, Karin, hails. He once told me that Karin's family, the Poteckis, were royalty, until the forties when the Soviets came and dismantled their country and crushed anything that was royal in it. So the Poteckis went west and settled in this city in this new country and made their money from selling furs and knock-off courtly furniture to local aristocrats. When Karin married Sebastian they felt she had married down, he, far too slovenly and decent a man, far too perfectly unambitious for them to consider worthy of their Karin, and Karin apparently said to her family, fine, that's okay, if I never see you all again I don't care, Sebastian is a good man and I love him and I will spend my life with him. I try to imagine this ardent woman, but she merely morphs into Bettina from a decade ago, on the night I first met her in a pub during a summer music festival in my hometown. I saw her near the back of a bar, late on a warm raucous night. She had bobbed light-brown hair, large blue eyes and fine lightly muscled and tanned arms. She was sipping from a glass of beer and I knew she was only passing through and that I would most likely never see her again, so I talked to her. Later, as we drunkenly stumbled down a laneway, she led me into a front garden and pushed me under a tree, pulled my trousers down, lifted her denim skirt and lowered herself onto me, and said, 'Please, please don't come.'

Having not had sex in over three years, I came long and thoroughly. After I stopped panting, she bent down and kissed my mouth, deeply and softly, and said she was not getting off until I really fucked her. She need not have worried – I was young – and within minutes we screwed again under that tree, and as she whispered and groaned and her shoulders shook under the canopy of the willow, I came once more, in threads, hundreds of them. Thus, I believe, Horst.

Six months later I moved to her city, this one I now call home, this one I am an hour outside, my headlights merely registering the moth-wing flares of snow swooning onto my path.

I arrive at a bungalow, and because I cannot believe this is a farm, I pull in to enquire as to the farm's whereabouts. A middle-aged lady with recently dyed dark hair comes to the door and I ask where the farm with the honey is, where the Bergs live, and she smiles, looks at me sideways and says, 'Are you Sebastian's man?'

'Yes,' I say enthusiastically.

She disappears into the kitchen and reappears moments later carrying four twelve-pot packs of golden honey, each pot with a red lid, and on the side of each pot, a pale blue sticker with the words BERG HONEY printed in austere white capitals.

I leave, put the pots of honey under a thick shaggy blanket on the back seats of the van and clamber behind the steering wheel. Before I start up the engine again, I sit in the white glow of the snow around me and think about the apartment

Bettina and I live in with our four boys. I recall the time Sebastian visited to pick me up for a drink so we could celebrate a book review I had had published the week before in a worthwhile if little-read journal in London. When we got to the pub – a small smoky place four streets away, it was raining and the cobbles were slick – we sat at the bar and the Turkish owner, Frank, approached for our order. Sebastian told him why we were celebrating. Frank furnished our beers with two shot glasses of schnapps, which we downed together, and just as we clinked our beer glasses Sebastian looked to me and said, 'You need a bigger place.'

'I know,' I said, averting my eyes, 'I know.'

I peer out at the Berg's yellow windows, rub my hands together, start up Sebastian's van and ease onto the slip road. My breath puffs and blooms before me, like small brains of vapour that dissipate slowly as I trundle along. The going is terrible and when I turn onto the main road leading back into the city, the carriageway appears utterly desolate and the madness of this trip becomes clear to me. I bring the van to a near-standstill. The snow is coming down so thickly that I can barely see the boundless dark beyond it, so I begin to pull in, but it is too late. A huge truck is sliding sidelong towards me. It is moving so patiently, so quietly, so inevitably at me that I merely cower and wait until the mother-elephant shunt arrives, and when it does nothing breaks or shatters or crushes, but I feel that I have immediately changed direction, smoothly, inexorably, backwards and to the right until the whole van tips over and I am upside down, tumbling, with an aching slowness into the white, and as I roll, incrementally, over and over, I promise to get a bigger place for my kids, away from the planes, away from the four small beds in our tiny second bedroom, away from the bin collector's alarm clock and away from Sebastian. Then, the muffled tumbling stops and I am lying upside down with my back pressed against the cold windscreen of the van, totally still, and as I wait for the next shiver or rotation or groan I can see that many of the pots of honey are broken and their contents are oozing across the seats above me.

9

We Too Have Wind-blown Plazas

Years back, I worked as an engineer in Dublin. I designed large buildings throughout the trembling city. These animals would unfold dustily to the sky, where they yawned, stretched, bellowed, then settled down to sleep. Then we'd go out and celebrate our labours; we would eat steak and drink red wine.

When all of this stopped, I moved to Abu Dhabi to work. I promised myself I would never return.

I wanted to perish in the desert.

•

The consultancy I worked for in Abu Dhabi was employed by a Mr Van der Woude – a tall Belgian with a mane of thick blond hair. He'd made his money as an hotelier in

Antwerp and Brussels, and had a reputation for attention to detail, spending days examining all sources of expenditure, from the reinforcement in the foundations up to the type of font on the penthouse apartment doors. He studied engineering as a younger man so I couldn't bamboozle him with jargon when he kept me behind after the weekly meetings to have me justify my designs. If these at times lengthy meetings went well, he'd take me out for lunch in a restaurant across town. If a meeting displeased him, he would sit across the table from me and roll his tongue around in his mouth, then dismiss me. Sometimes I'd catch glimpses of him pounding around our district of Abu Dhabi talking and gesturing expansively among groups of pristinely turned-out Emirate businessmen.

Otherwise, working weeks and months and seasons passed with an intense singularity. Van der Woude's building was eighty storeys and such was the poor quality of construction that my time was consumed with troublesome repairs all the way up the structure. At first I spent my weekends with other Western engineers, all of whom had interchangeably pleasant young families, but the polite familial conservativeness began to bore me, and after a while I found myself spending weekends on my own. I stopped drinking to focus on my work. I saw opportunity in my application to Van der Woude's hotel.

By then I'd lost contact with my father, my estranged mother, my friends and any old colleagues back home. On quiet evenings in my apartment, I'd recall the last day I spent with my father while my mother and he were still together.

They were sitting at the kitchen table that morning as I wandered into the adjacent sitting room, unnoticed, and my father, mid-sentence and turning towards my mother, said, '... he's such a limited boy really, he seems to make the world simpler to better fit it to his mind. I wish he'd open himself out into the chaos of it all.'

My mother didn't reply, and I don't know if it was that she could feel I was near or if she did not agree.

Later that evening as my father dropped me into town, I asked him what he had meant.

He at first denied saying it, then claimed I had misinterpreted, then, he relented. 'It's just talk,' he shrugged, 'your mother and I ... She wants to leave. I wanted to remind her that I could still be insightful, or something.'

'Jesus,' I said.

'I am sorry.'

I looked over at him, his hunched shoulders, his soft hands, his balding pate.

'Stop the car.'

'Relax,' he replied, 'we're nearly there.'

'Pull over. I'll walk.'

'Foster, please, the road is too –'

But I'd already thrown myself out the door, and was tumbling into a ditch. I came to that night in hospital, covered in bruises, with a broken arm and a shattered knee. My mother was stroking my hair, smiling at me. Her blue eyes were wet.

By the time I could hobble my parents had gone their separate ways, the summer was over and I was going back to university for my final year. My mother, in love, cut contact with us, and my father dissolved into a panel-beaten version of himself and our relationship thinned to occasional emails and texts. We all strayed, in that depressingly mature and adult way, in three different directions. It was a sort of drift that only death or grave illness can interrupt.

•

During lunch one day, in the last few weeks of the hotel project, I was sitting, in a tinkling restaurant, across from Van der Woude, who was chewing emphatically on a large leaf salad. Over his shoulder, stands of high-rises receded into the hazy distance. Cranes swivelled on top of these structures, delicately lifting materials up and down. Though it was smoggy I could still make out tiny shimmering men in yellow hard hats darting around these distant floors carrying out their work in slowly making real another person's roaring dream. Van der Woude put his knife down and said that he considered me a fine engineer, and that I'd done good work for him.

'You should visit me in my apartment some evening,' he said, as he forked a cherry tomato, '… if you have nothing else to do.'

I called up the following Friday. His apartment was on the sixtieth floor of an obnoxiously vertical building across town. I was greeted at the door of the apartment by a stout Filipino lady, in her late forties, and who was dressed in a neatly pressed black-and-white uniform. She led me into a cool and expansive living room, fringed with wobbling tropical plants. Van der Woude was reclined on an antique chaise longue, reading a *National Geographic*. He wore tracksuit bottoms, flip-flops and a silken green dressing gown. He asked the housekeeper to leave and to bring his black cat too. He told me that it was in must and had been mewling horribly at its own reflection all day. He then bade me sit next to him and offered me a beer, which I at first refused, but he insisted, so I gave in, and, at his further insistence, I relaxed. Befriending him, I thought, would serve me well. We drank a number of beers and chit-chatted about the city, his hotel and the plans he had for more. Then, he reached forward and from under the coffee table he produced a dark Tupperware tub, filled with tiny plastic bags of pills and white powder. He enquired if I'd ever taken class-As before.

'I have not,' I said.

We took MDMA with a little librium; it was fucking extraordinary. Hours later we were laughing on the couch. My mind had voided upward, heavenward, foreverward. My pupils were rolling back in my eyes – like small breaking tides – and my mouth gurned, ground and chewed on dry, salty cud. I was grinning extravagantly at Van der Woude, who was regaling me about the sex clubs he used to visit in Belgium as a younger man. He said he missed that free and blissful part of his life dearly.

I shook my head, gazed out over the twinkling tubes of the city, took a sip of beer and said, 'You're some man.' Then I rose from the couch, turned up the techno that had been thudding softly through the room and I began to dance.

Hours later as I was leaving his apartment, he called after me. 'Stay a while longer. I have some grass; we can come down together,' he said.

He was standing at the entrance to his sitting room sipping tea. He put the cup down, stalked back into the room and slipped out of his clothes. He unfurled his thickening white body onto the chaise longue, shook out his hair and arranged himself onto his side, propped up on pillows with his right hand to the fore, the left resting across his genitals. Then he fixed his gaze olympically out at me. His cat sprang onto the foot of the chaise longue, and the Filipino lady appeared behind him drawing the curtains across the window. This image flickered in my mind as I turned and left. His apartment door then swung to behind me, and in that moment between the click-clump of the door closing and the ping of the hall lights flickering on, I stood, suspended in the cool humming darkness of the corridor, itself tracing a truncated architectural trajectory through the early morning sky I had momentarily just become.

I took a taxi across town to my apartment where I sat out on my balcony, twelve storeys up. I looked towards the sun rising in the east. The buildings glinted, and on the ground, way below, the shadows of these towers folded themselves across each other. I had no idea how far east I was. I yearned for some energy, but I was already succumbing to sleep. My eyelids drooped and the dawn breeze slowed to a near standstill. I felt it creep across my forehead while sucking sweat beads from my pores. I drew on a cigarette and fell further back into my body, my spine, my buttocks, through the straining deckchair canvas and into the floor and walls of my apartment until I felt myself coalescing with the entire building. Then I filled the building, every floor, every corridor, every room and every shoe in every room with an Amazonian inhalation of smoke. The smoke-cloud lingered and curled into the air-conditioning currents swirling through the space; then, I exhaled brutally, voiding the structure. Everything left behind created reverbs through my body. I felt the breeze meet the surface of the windward face of the building, over and again, then moments later I felt the suction of these passing breezes on the leeward face as they gathered around and tugged gently at the back of my neck, dissipating shudders from the top of the structure all the way down to the ground. I felt every beam and column translate these deflections and surface resonances into multitudes of smaller vectors that advanced inward to the lift shaft of the building where these forces and ideas of forces were absorbed, subsumed, then guided down along the calcifying grid-lines of the lift shaft's abstract pre-history, onward, slowing, downward, crawling, towards a dark and wet subterranean bedrock where all of this was stilled to nothing against the gorgeous inertia of the earth.

•

Within a month my contract had finished and I'd turned
down a renewal. I had accrued some savings so I stayed on
in my place to kick back during the week, enjoy some time
off, go to driving ranges and hit balls, visit the cinema, and
every Friday I'd call around to Van der Woude. Each time,
I took greater doses and as the weeks passed he'd propose
different cocktails. I think he enjoyed my increasingly
addled reactions.

I asked him once, during one of our binges, why no one
else ever came.

To which he smiled benevolently across the room, 'I've
worked closely with you, Foster. I trust you. I've seen one
side of your personality. Now, I am interested to see the rest.
You seem to me to be alone, and I am too, amongst so much
plenty, and I find this very beautiful. But also,' he continued,
now laughing gently, 'I want to help you realize yourself.'

A few months later, on a Saturday morning at around two, a
Thai call girl arrived. I was so epically strung out that all I
could do was sit in an easy chair and hold onto its arms for
dear life as I looked on with horror at Van der Woude have
sex expertly, endlessly, with this call girl on his couch. Hours
later as the drugs eased into an expansive mellow I felt like I
could try standing up. My eyes returned from searching the
dark firmament of my skull, and I could see Van der Woude,
grinning broadly now, recline, with the call girl sitting on

his lap, she smoking a cigarette. Then he slipped his head behind her torso, splayed his arms either side and passed out.

I blinked and when I opened my eyes, the beautiful Thai woman was before me gently pulling my trousers down over my knees. After many minutes of trying to give me head she looked up and said, 'Your dick is dead.'

Van der Woude was snoring on the couch. He looked dishevelled, disastrous and suddenly very old. I realized he was the sort of man that my father would disdain. I left.

While traversing the quiet streets back towards my apartment I felt an urge to go for a swim. The sun was rising and I could feel the heat growing. I walked past empty high rises and on through stilled building sites, then further, to the slums that surrounded the beach. Hundreds of Pakistani, Indian and Burmese men were emerging from their tents and walking towards buses to shuttle them to a site. I fingered a pill left over from Van der Woude's place and slipped it into my mouth, then I followed a group of labourers onto a bus, and we were driven back through the silver city, past tower blocks, shining half-domes of shopping villages, unfinished vulva-shaped football stadia.

The site we pulled in at was a grim concrete-framed thing that seemed decades from completion. We entered a broad passageway into a dark furnace-like floor and descended seven storeys in a rattling lift to the pit of the building. Dozens of half-naked men of slight build were strewn across the grey puddled floor, asleep, and in the far corner gaped a huge hole through which water cascaded. Four men were shot-spraying concrete at it, as if they were trying to put out a fire. A sheet of reinforcement bent away from the wall. The men brandishing the hose roared. One of them looked to me and he, thinking I was the site manager and that he had ought to appear dutiful in front of me, approached the wall and pushed the reinforcement back in place as the others covered it and him with concrete. I raced across to cajole him away, but he would not move. I retreated and watched him being covered over with this thumping stream of wet cement, and I thought that he would soon certainly die. I asked the men to cease their work, but they would not listen. I stood back and watched the bending grey torrent through my fingers. Just as I thought this man was lost to the wall he peeled himself away and rejoined the men behind the hose. I slumped to the ground and waited. The man covered in concrete then walked off. I followed him across the basement and up twenty flights of stairs until he turned onto an empty floor. I could see, through a massive unglazed opening, a large hexagon-shaped plaza below – it dotted out with shivering palm trees – connecting this tower to its brother. The sun was high in the sky and the heat was horrible. The light wobbled through a horizontal slit of white and orange. I was sweating and dangerously out of breath as I chased after the man covered in concrete. Then he slowed, stopped and in mid-step completely hardened over. I ran to him calling for help but there was no one around so I tried to break the concrete off with my fingers, but it was too hard. I looked into his eyes for any sign of life, but they were totally still.

I punched his face till my knuckles bled; then, I searched for a crowbar or a drill or anything that might break a breathing hole in the concrete, but I could find nothing so I took a run and shoved him over. He toppled and split in two. I shrieked and ran and ran down through the building and out into the chaotic workspaces below, chasing from the buildings until the land opened. I found a concrete pit into which I clambered, panting and pouring with sweat. I paced in a circle for many minutes then lay down in a slant of shadow.

When I woke it was night, and I was cold. I looked to the sky – nothing. I pulled my phone from my pocket, called the police and told them what had happened. I was dithering, ravenous and parched.

They found grass in my pocket, and brought me to a police station where I sat for three days and nights thinking about this split concrete man, and then, I thought of my father, sitting alone in his house. I realized I not only despised home up close, but now I also despised it from afar. And I realized that the time I'd spent in Abu Dhabi was merely an avoidance of this rage I'd felt accumulating before I'd even left home, and it occurred to me too, sitting in that overheated cell, that it was a sort of anger that I had tried for years to shrink with the scale of the constructions I helped to erect around it, believing that making it irrelevant might make it go away. But in doing this, I realized I'd learned nothing new about the nature of this anger towards my father and the country to which he belongs, other than that this anger had not become less fierce and that it still badly needed somewhere to go, and, as I stood up in this police cell, it occurred to me that this rage would never be vented back home.

A day later I was released and escorted to the airport. I asked after my belongings and my apartment. They informed me that the embassy would make contact once I was home. I was told that I was a lucky man and that I should never try entering this country again.

I was handed my phone and immediately rang Van der Woude. I wanted him to tell me everything was okay, but the number rang out. I tried again and he answered, 'Foster?'

'The police,' I said, 'I got caught with some –'

But he'd already hung up. I rang again, then again, but there was no connection. I opened the phone and, peering in at its tiny microchips, networks and nodes, I tried to remember something of the building I'd helped him build, but it fell away into every other building whose innards I'd come to know.

I sat back on the concourse bench between my two police escorts and waited for the delegate from the embassy to arrive. I looked around and realized the airport building was almost unrecognizable to when I first came here. The departures area was now throbbing: men in business suits on laptops; drowsy women with headscarves, fanning themselves, festooned with fabric and children; makeshift beds of normalized nomads strewn in corners; herds of ageing Americans; dozing, tanned and nubile young Westerners slumped uncomfortably on plastic seats; and old grey-bearded men in knee-length shirts and loose trousers, with round flat hats on their heads, sitting up and staring blankly at the dazzling central core of the airport, where text feeds of international news bites scrolled, interspersed with adverts, football clips and flight-information updates. I imagined those men, forty, fifty, sixty years ago as youths sitting somewhere in some small sandy village street squinting and wondering what on earth to do and where to do it; then, with my head in my hands, I thought of my father sitting in a glass-walled coffee house, in a quiet commercial development deposited off an unfinished roundabout outside his helpless hometown in the southern Midlands, completing a crossword and occasionally drinking from an over-sized mug of frothy milk, and peering up every now and then to eye the handsome dark-haired waitress on the cusp of growing sugar thick around the waist, and imagining, in between the black gaps of the nearly words he diligently re-constructs on the page, the things he would like to do to her, of an afternoon, in a room in the old Railway Hotel in the centre of town, amid the fust, the faux-Victorian-patterned crunch of carpet and the faint spiralling scents of sad old sex and tissue drifting out the sash-window overlooking a street of cars, child-buggies, waste, people and their rage, or something that sounds like rage, but rage that has been continuously doused and beaten and bent and broken, until it is barely even rage at all.

COACH

About the Weight of a Bucket of Salt

Vincent, a young artist from Dublin, moved to Berlin in the early nineties. During the previous decade he'd briefly attended Hamburg's Academy of Fine Arts as an exchange student, where he'd befriended an up-and-coming gallerist called Albert. It was one of those easy friendships people often make in their late teens; friendships that people can pick up and enjoy through their lives no matter how infrequently they meet. When Vincent returned to Ireland to complete his studies, Albert promised, should Vincent ever return to Germany, that they would get together and put on some shows.

In the intervening years Vincent's practice moved from photography towards sculpture, and when they met again, Albert was unconvinced by this shift, because it had been

Vincent's black-and-white photographs of building sites, playgrounds and zoos that had initially so impressed him.

Vincent said he'd take an atelier in Berlin for six months and, if the new sculptures were not to Albert's liking, he would either leave Berlin or return to photography and develop a body of work for Albert to show. Albert agreed, but after a number of weeks sitting in his cavernous studio — once the offices of a long-defunct brewery — Vincent realized he did not want to work indoors, so he cancelled his lease and took to trawling the streets each day, loading a trolley with scraps of building material and other fragments of the crumbling city's jetsam. When he collected enough, he'd find space in one of the many empty industrial buildings around north-east Berlin, and secretly fashion a sculpture. Within a fortnight he had ten new sculptures in ten empty buildings dotted around north Prenzlauer Berg, Weissensee, Pankow. Vincent rang Albert immediately, telling him he believed these sculptures to be his finest work and that he should come to Berlin as soon as possible to view them.

Albert arrived a week later. They strode along desolate thoroughfares, courtyards and through decaying buildings that seemed to barely remember how to stay upright. Over the course of their walk, Vincent and Albert found five of the sculptures had been dismantled, tampered with irreparably or stripped for firewood. One had all but disappeared. Four of the remaining works left Albert uninterested, even frustrated, because they seemed to him little more than drab rehearsals of a style of abstract sculpture he had seen hundreds of times before. One work, however, at the far end of a crumbling six-storey warehouse in Pankow, left Albert completely wordless. The sun had come out, and because this warehouse had no roof, light poured onto the joists and trusses and floorboards, across the walls and the other desiccated innards of the building and onto Vincent's sculpture: a small shack, made with dark timber panels and sheets of steel, with a lean-to roof, one square window, a door and around the perimeter innumerable shards of broken glass bottles that twinkled in the sun like ice flowers. Vincent and Albert stared at the sculpture shimmering in the shafts of sunlight, it made strangely homely by the enormous god-forsaken warehouse sheltering it. Then they left without uttering a word until they found a small *Bäckerei* where, warmed by their coffees, Albert congratulated Vincent on the whole endeavour.

Ambling back through the city towards the main train station, Albert said to Vincent that if he photographed this work he'd happily exhibit and sell the prints in his gallery in Hamburg. But Vincent claimed he would be unable to do this, venturing that 'such an act would be an insult to the structures of subtlety offered by the physical encounter of the works', and to photograph it, he insisted, 'would be nothing short of pounding the whole thing into the ground.'

Albert returned to Hamburg, miffed. In the following weeks he wrote to Vincent a number of times asking him to document this work, but Vincent, enthral to the idea of the ephemeral art object, resisted, saying in his final letter that he 'had moved on to new things'.

Albert contacted a young graduate, whose work he'd seen in a group show in Cologne a few months before – a dozen grimy inkjet prints of a metal bridge in Haßfurt – and asked him to reinterpret Vincent's arresting object in Berlin. The photographer produced eight large prints of this shack, and six months later Albert exhibited them in his gallery, under the title 'Found House'.

Vincent was furious. He travelled to Hamburg a number of times to confront Albert, and such was the scale of his rage that Albert had to request a restraining order from the *Polizei*. Vincent broke contact with Albert and that brief, fertile and happy period of his creative life came to an end.

Over the following years Vincent slumped, in almost imperceptible increments, away from the world of art and towards amateur chess and alcohol.

·

Ten years later and Vincent was standing in the middle of his handsome but ramshackle apartment with a letter in his hand stating that he must vacate it in a month – the building had been recently deemed unsafe. Thin and haggard, though he was only forty-two, he looked to be well into his fifties. His hair was grey and long and the central parting was no longer an adamant line splitting two seas of ginger-red, but now a crackling furrow of bent wobbling follicles. A touch of yellow had entered him. A lamp on the wall, its shade browned with smoke, threw angular shadows across the room. Vincent was all but naked; a pair of navy underpants hung from his hips. He sighed, then reached to the back of his armchair, lifted his coat from it, shook the coat out and threw it over his shoulders – and set about making breakfast. He sat at his kitchen table and sipped a coffee as he ate a stale biscuit, found at the bottom of a tin. The table, which was circular in shape, was covered in old newspapers and cuttings from books about chess.

He realized that he'd squandered his thirties.

He pictured the apotheosis – a night spent in a jail cell for attacking an old college-friend called Kurt, an acclaimed video artist, who Vincent believed to have acted dishonourably some years previous while Vincent was seeing a youthful American postdoc he loved called Suzi. That drunken night in Vincent's local bar, he confronted Kurt claiming it was Kurt's promptings that had driven Suzi from him.

While Kurt was married to his first wife, Katrin, the four of them would go out often for food and drinks. During these competitively playful evenings, while Katrin and Vincent were engaged in conversation, Kurt would stare at Suzi, his stately blue eyes trying to eke from her a flicker of sexual desire. Kurt often re-directed conversation towards Vincent and Katrin, in an attempt to carve out this quiet space for he and Suzi – one he assumed Suzi would happily venture into. He would have liked nothing more than to fuck Suzi on the table in front of Katrin and Vincent as they chatted inanely to each other, such was the bored infantile disdain with which he held his wife and his colleague.

Over the weeks and months, Kurt created an atmosphere at the table that though once mysterious and exciting soon congealed. When Suzi brought this up with Vincent, he decided to bring this four-way friendship to an end. For the next three weeks, Vincent and Kurt awkwardly thrust conversation over and back at each other, until their last meal together, when Vincent relented – and as he spoke with Katrin about a show Kurt mentioned that she'd seen somewhere in Leipzig, Kurt stared quietly at Suzi; and Vincent, as he spoke to Katrin, slowly turned his head to Kurt, saying, with obvious malevolence, 'Is there something you want, Kurt?'

These slights resurfaced the night of the assault in Vincent's local pub when Vincent, sloppily drunk, tried to glass Kurt's face, but he missed and was pulled to the ground, and Kurt pressed full charges of ABH, which, when eventually heard in court, the judge, a sincere woman in her late thirties, threw out as preposterous, vain, small.

With the whitening mid-morning light breaking through the windows of his apartment and falling across the available angles of his aspect, Vincent erected himself, bone by bone, and reached for his small notebook. As if he had been sitting there for many years, plumes of dust twisted into the air, then fell. He pulled his telephone out from under a mound of coats and, consulting his notebook, rang Albert, who – after some confusion, queries, missed connections and further calls – rang back, and though he and Vincent engaged in a terse conversation at first, he agreed to meet him at his new gallery in Charlottenburg the next day.

The day was cold but Vincent decided to cycle. His ravaged tweed coat flapped out behind him as he pedalled elegantly through the broad streets and the sleet towards Albert's gallery, it flanked by two glass-fronted spaces, one dotted with large monochrome paintings, the other with a 16-millimetre projector playing, in reverse, archival footage of men assembling a Ford Model T.

Inside Albert's gallery, misshapen clumps of concrete sat on purple-, black- and pink-coloured pools of sand. Vincent peered past the artworks and waved at Albert standing by a reception desk conversing with a slim and blond adolescent. Albert, with his thick dark hair, had barely aged since Vincent last saw him.

'Vincent!' Albert called cheerfully, 'come in!'

Vincent wound his way past the artworks and up to Albert, who looked carefully at Vincent, taking in his clothes and physical state. Then Albert embraced him warmly. Vincent, overcome, began to cry. Albert looked to the young beautiful receptionist and gestured that he make a pot of tea, then ushered Vincent into his bright back-room office. Albert pulled up a chair, sat Vincent down and whispered, while rubbing his back, 'There there, old friend, there there.'

Then, into the strange quiet that filled Albert's office, stepped the adolescent with a pot of tea and two pewter cups. He poured the tea, as Vincent's sobbing lifted once more, to which Albert gestured to this slim adolescent to leave.

Vincent's sobbing ebbed. He took a sip from the steaming cup, coughed and blurted, 'Albert, I need your help. I'm to be evicted from my apartment next month.'

Albert shifted in his chair and took a sip from his cup too. 'What will you do?' he asked.

'You owe me, Albert.'

Albert said nothing.

He detected how his old slight had propped Vincent's life up. He detected also that it was the only thing of value left to him, and how this perceived injustice had permitted Vincent's dissolution from himself.

A silence bloomed between them. Then, a bird chirped outside.

'Are you still making work, Vincent?'

Vincent peered at Albert imploringly.

They fell back into silence for many moments, until the young receptionist came to the door. He looked at them both, then, unnoticed, walked away. Albert rose and took a catalogue from a shelf behind his desk. It was one by the photographer who'd captured Vincent's house-sculpture all those years ago. Vincent flicked through the book and Albert recounted, with no heat, how this photographer's career had progressed and that he had left them last year for a larger gallery in New York. Vincent eventually came upon the eight black-and-white prints of his sculpture. He slowed, then said to Albert that they were very fine photographs but hostile, in principle, to the nature of the original work.

'It was quite a while ago,' said Albert.

'It was,' said Vincent.

'My friend, where precisely is your accommodation?'

'Auguststraße.'

'*Gott*, Vincent,' Albert sighed, extending his hands towards him, 'you must know that the whole *Kiez* is being bought up. You must know all of those squats you people live in will soon be gone.'

Vincent looked down at his feet, then back to Albert.

'You were a moderate artist, Vincent, in a silly young city. I could've made you a moderate career, but you ... and now you turn up here like this. I speak kindly; leave your place and find somewhere inexpensive before it is too late. If you get yourself in order and find an atelier, I promise I will visit and see what I can do.'

Vincent stood, then straightened, 'A squat, you say.'

He left, cycled back to his apartment and removed his clothes. As he padded across the twilight of his room he rubbed the slackened skin of his stomach. For the first time in years he thought of home, his family in Ireland, his parents, who died within a fortnight of each other fifteen years before, and his older brother who had spent the last twenty years sequestered in a monastery in rural Cork. Vincent, standing still in the still darkness of this apartment yearned for the sea. He lay onto his bed and pulled his bedclothes over his body and, as the dusk gathered around him and disappeared in languorous blinks, he resolved that when he woke he would set about leaving this part of the city.

Next morning he rose early and went to the *Konditorei* on the corner. Sitting at the window, sipping his espresso, he took in the bicycles and pedestrians rushing by. He purchased a packet of black bags and set about clearing up his apartment, stacking to one side of his kitchen-cum-bedroom some books and smaller artworks he'd been gifted over the years. Amid these belongings he found a photograph of Suzi and he sitting on a staircase at a party, surrounded by strangers. They both held stubby glasses of red wine and were smiling. Her dark hair was cropped up short, and her beautiful dark eyes were trained on something in the near distance. A strange regretlessness simmered up. He remembered meeting her at a film screening in a friend's house, their first few dates and the intensity of their time together when they moved into this place – the eternal romantic excitement of it all. He remembered her appetite for sex too, and the private promiscuity she had towards their love life. It fascinated him; but this difference between them then only marked him out as a conservative sexual partner, which she at first found sweet, then boring, then pointless. He held, now, however, only pornographic memories of her, memories he still pleasured himself to – his buttocks quietly beating his member into the inert gloaming of his fist, fantasizing, from an unlikely place, her soft limbs, her groans – memories he knew no longer had any correspondence to his experience of her. For eight years he'd been buckled by these fantasies. Every day he had tended to a woman he pushed further from actuality or existence. Vincent was disappointed for misremembering her in this way, and for his misuse of the good of what is gradual in love and life.

Later that evening he returned to his apartment with two lamb chops, a handful of potatoes and a newspaper. After dinner he scanned the classifieds for apartments, circling one offering a room for thirty euro a week. It was a third-floor apartment up north, somewhere in the Scandinavian Quarter. The viewings for the apartment were scheduled from seven the next day.

That night, the weather became cold. Snow fell in waves and drifts. The city grew quiet again. Vincent visited his local bar, a twenty-four-hour place that sheltered punks and transients who lived in freezing and poorly plumbed *altbau* buildings like his and liked a late drink. He stayed until six in the morning with his heroically bearded friend Manfred, a retired typesetter from the old West. Manfred and Vincent gleefully posited a theory over the course of the night – as they reminisced about Berlin and the speed at which it was being re-constructed – that these new buildings popping up all over the cityscape were merely new kinds of publications, 'monumental publications albeit', as Vincent described them. Near the end of the night as they reached their conclusions, Manfred, with some finality, raised a finger in the air and woozily declared over the ebbing thrum of the pub, 'The only real typesetters left in this city, dear Vincent, are therefore the tower-crane operators,' and his finger fell into his fist, which he dropped to the table with a bang, 'witness them plunging their enormous steel letters into the soil!' And to this theatre Vincent whooped, cackled and clapped.

Next evening, Vincent viewed the apartment. It was suitable, so, a few days later he moved in with a bag of clothes, a folder of paper, his old Hasselblad camera and three books – short-story collections by Doris Lessing that Suzi had given him for his thirty-fourth birthday. He'd read these stories so many times and enjoyed the feeling of the books in his hands so much that he couldn't bear to leave them with the rest of his belongings, bundled up miscellaneously in two sacks outside his old apartment building.

Within a few months Vincent began working at a nearby pub, a busy corner *Kneipe* that filled with labourers each evening from six until late, but was quiet and peaceful during the earlier hours. He put on a little weight, and ate more regularly, his cheeks filled out and his hair, though cut up short, thickened and reddened again. He had taken some new photographs too, of the old East German embassies that circled nearby Stavanger Straße – Communist cubes of concrete and glass, housing countries like Moldova, Cuba, Eritrea, Ghana, the Cape Verde Islands.

One night he went out to photograph the lamps around the square, just as they fluttered from purple to their sombre orange glow. He was fiddling with his tripod when a black woman strode past in a long fur coat, and she asked him if he was gazing at the stars.

'No,' he replied, 'the lamps.'

She looked up at the disc-shaped lamp, it glowing there like a low-flying UFO.

'If you go west of here, just over the bridge, the lamps are entirely different,' she said, 'they are bell-shaped and their glow is paler.'

'Do you live here?' asked Vincent.

'In the Ghanaian embassy.'

'Is it nice?'

'I've been here years,' she replied almost mournfully. 'Are you a photographer?'

'I'm an artist,' said Vincent, as he peered down into the eyepiece of his camera.

'Photograph me,' she said.

Vincent smiled, 'What's your name?'

'Elizabeth. You?'

'Vincent. Please go to that lamp, into the circle of light at its base and raise your face a little.'

She posed beside the lamppost as Vincent rearranged his tripod.

'Please keep still; the exposure is twelve seconds,' he said.

She stood beneath the lamp, her chin lifted, this beautiful Elizabeth, for twelve seconds, in total silence, then once the shutter clicked closed, she nodded, and bade him a pleasant night.

When Vincent developed the roll he was pleased with the photographs of the embassies and the lamps. The photograph of Elizabeth, however, was somewhat soft, fuzzy and a little too bright.

'She must have moved,' he said aloud as he inspected the image.

From the photographic prints of the embassies he made delicate black-and-white collages, realizing as he worked that collaging in this way was itself a sculpting of time and pattern into appealing new compositions populating new time and pattern.

Upon completing six works he contacted Albert. He made a folio from plywood and felt, and one morning in early spring he cycled over to the gallery. Albert loved the collages, and offered to have all of them framed for exhibition in a group show he was organizing the following July.

'Wonderful, Vincent, wonderful,' he muttered as they pored over the small but expert works.

Cycling home, Vincent felt strangely empty. He stopped at Auguststraße to see how his old building looked, but it was completely shrouded in pink dust-drapes, and was full of builders. He rolled along to a café at the end of the street and as he stood outside sipping a tea, he looked at the dark boughs of the linden tree above him. He saw the green buds slicing their way out into their small soon-to-be-summer expanses.

He thought of his lungs.

The butcher's across the way had been replaced with a discreet commercial art gallery. He wandered over. The place was empty and bright, with three tastefully framed photographs of serene mid-ocean waves hung along the right-hand wall. Underneath, a shin-high triangle of white neon tubing leaned against the wall, and to the rear he spied a gleaming metal bucket sitting on the polished concrete floor. He walked to the bucket and peered in – it was full of rough sea salt. He fell silent as he circled the bucket, over and over, drawn in by the centrifugal quietnesses of this small island of metal and sodium. He wanted to pick the bucket up and feel its heft, but he knew if he did, he would ruin everything memorable about it.

His mediocrity as an artist became apparent to him.

He left, and pedalled back up the Schönhauser-Allee hill to work.

That evening, during a quiet moment behind the bar, he wrote to Albert asking him not to bother framing or showing his competent new collages – 'to scrap the whole idea completely'. Instead, Vincent suggested they meet someday soon for a drink and a couple of cigarettes.

A few weeks later, Vincent, still troubled by the poorly executed photograph he took of Elizabeth, decided to visit the embassy to see if he could propose a re-shoot.

Elizabeth greeted him at the door and invited him into a meeting room filled with the scent of freshly polished timber. Vincent produced the print. The photo had been taken from a position lower than what is usual in portraiture, and this, coupled with the stately confidence of Elizabeth's stance – draped in fur, framed by the dark, the street lamp glowing like a halo above her – gave the image a kitsch and ethereally regal quality.

'*Très* pop-video,' she beamed. 'I love it.'

Vincent, who was about to apologize for the picture's many flaws merely smiled, saying, 'Then, please have it.'

Elizabeth left to make them coffee. Vincent reclined and as the chair creaked gently beneath him he took in the various pieces of traditional and modern Ghanaian art: wall-mounted textiles, masks, photographs of modernist buildings edged out in red-and-yellow chevrons, pictures of beaches and paintings of sunsets. The colours and patterns entranced him.

When Elizabeth returned with a clinking tray, he asked her about travelling to Ghana.

A year later and Vincent is lying alone on a vast bright beach on the far outskirts of Accra. The sun is out and a breeze skips along the shore whipping sand and rustling the leaves of the giant palms behind him. He's just finished a joint fashioned from local grass, the sort that leads him daily into mild hallucination.

In the evenings he fishes, then he sleeps in a small grass-roofed bungalow he bought in exchange for his Hasselblad. He speaks sometimes to the locals, purchasing food and books, but by and large his life revolves around a game he plays with himself each day at four in the afternoon when he ventures out into the sea for a swim. It's a game of balance between the pleasure of swimming in this salty water and the inertia of being well and truly stoned. Sometimes, as he floats on his back, he has visions – the sky often opens before him, revealing celestial spectra of breathtaking beauty. Each day, he inches himself into a more profound high before going for his swim. Perfection, he reckons, will be the day he is too weak to float and too mashed to panic.

He is slim and his hair is sun-bleached almost white. His eyes have shrunken from sunken pebbles to mere dots. His skin is still brightly pale as if no amount of sun will ever alter it. Lying on the sand, he breathes deeply, exhaling a last tendril of smoke; then he rises and walks unsteadily out to the sea, wading one more time into the disintegrating rolls of advancing surf.

Acknowledgments

The bucket-of-salt artwork that appears in the story 'About the Weight of a Bucket of Salt' takes its inspiration from an artwork by the Irish artist David Beattie titled 'Static' (2013), first exhibited in the group show *Solitude. In no particular order* (2013) at the Goethe-Institut Irland in Dublin.

Thank you to:
Ruth Hallinan, Don Duncan, Brendan Barrington, Rebecca O'Connor, Sally Rooney, Aoife Walsh, Helen Chandler, Susan Tomaselli, Feargal Ward, Dr Francis Halsall, Anna Benn, Wendy Erskine, Marianne Gunn O'Connor, Nora Hickey M'Sichili, The Joinery, The Irish Writers Centre, Centre Culturel Irlandais, *Literature Ireland*, *The Dublin Review*, *The Stinging Fly*, *The Moth*, *Műűt*, Longford

Town FC, NCAD (ACW), IADT Dún Laoghaire, Clare Quinlan, Paul Gregg, Niall de Buitléar, Michelle Browne, Marta Fernández Calvo, Júlia Rácz, Miranda Driscoll, Peter Curran, Fabian and, of course, to my family.

Particular thanks also to Greg Baxter.

My gratitude to the Arts Council of Ireland from whom I received visual-artist bursaries while writing this book.

Thank you, as always, to Antony Farrell for the belief and encouragement – and all of the Lilliput Press team and board too.

And finally, my thanks to Seán Farrell, who edited this book.

Versions of some stories appeared in the following:

'Design No. 108', *Dublin Review* 52, Autumn 2013.
  Editor: Brendan Barrington.
'Midfield Dynamo', *Dublin Review* 57, Winter 2014.
  Editor: Brendan Barrington.
'Two Towers in a Forest', *Dublin Review* 59,
  Summer 2015. Editor: Brendan Barrington.
'Trusses', *Dublin Review* 65, Winter 2016. Editor:
  Brendan Barrington.
'Forty-eight Pots of Honey' (entitled 'Honey'), *The
  Moth*, Winter 2017. Editor: Rebecca O'Connor.
  This story also appeared in 2020 in the Hungarian
  literary journal *Műút* (translated by Júlia Rácz).
'Prosinečki', *The Stinging Fly*, Summer 2018. Editor:
  Sally Rooney.